先知【中英對照新版】

紀伯倫／著　　溫文慧／譯

The Prophet

By Kahlil Gibran

好讀出版

Table of contents 目錄

01 船的到來 THE COMING OF THE SHIP ／6

02 關於愛 ON LOVE ／22

03 關於婚姻 ON MARRIAGE ／28

04 關於孩子 ON CHILDREN ／32

05 關於施予 ON GIVING ／36

06 關於飲食 ON EATING AND DRINKING ／44

07 關於工作 ON WORK ／48

08 關於歡樂與憂愁 ON JOY AND SORROW ／56

09 關於房子 ON HOUSES ／60

10 關於衣服 ON CLOTHES ／68

11 關於買與賣 ON BUYING AND SELLING ／72

12 關於罪與罰 ON CRIME AND PUNISHMENT ／76

13 關於法律 ON LAWS / 88

14 關於自由 ON FREEDOM / 94

15 關於理性與熱情 ON REASON AND PASSION / 100

16 關於痛苦 ON PAIN / 104

17 關於自知 ON SELF-KNOWLEDGE / 108

18 關於教育 ON TEACHING / 112

19 關於友誼 ON FRIENDSHIP / 116

20 關於言談 ON TALKING / 120

21 關於時間 ON TIME / 124

22 關於善與惡 ON GOOD AND EVIL / 128

23 關於祈禱 ON PRAYER / 136

24 關於喜樂 ON PLEASURE / 142

25 關於美 ON BEAUTY / 150

26 關於宗教 ON RELIGION / 156

27 關於死亡 ON DEATH / 162

28 再會 THE FAREWELL / 166

4

The Prophet 先知

「紀伯倫詩作的魅力來自於某種強大的普世精神生活寶庫，但其詩之文字語言的美妙與莊嚴則全然得益於自身的天賦。」

克勞德・布萊登

01 船的到來

艾默斯塔法——被上天圈選且眷愛,是當代的曙光,他已在阿法利斯城等待了十二年,等著接他的船來到,要返回自己出生的小島。

而今正是第十二個年頭,在收割月的第七日,他爬上城牆外的山丘,眺望海面;在霧靄中遙見一艘船若隱若現地駛來。

他的心裡豁然開朗,喜樂飛越海洋。他閉上雙眼,祈禱著心靈獲得平靜。

當他爬下山丘時,卻有一股悲傷襲捲而來,心中默想著:

我該如何不帶任何一點悲傷,平靜地離別呢?喔,不,離開這城市,我豈能不傷痛呢?

在這城垣中,我度過多少獨自舔著傷痛,度過孤獨的夜晚;誰能因為揮別傷痛和寂寞而不心傷呢?

01

The Coming of the Ship

Almustafa, the chosen and the beloved, who was a dawn unto his own day, had waited twelve years in the city of Orphalese for his ship that was to return and bear him back to the isle of his birth.

And in the twelfth year, on the seventh day of Ielool, the month of reaping, he climbed the hill without the city walls and looked seaward; and he beheld the ship coming with the mist.

Then the gates of his heart were flung open, and his joy flew far over the sea. And he closed his eyes and prayed in the silences of his soul.

But he descended the hill, a sadness came upon him, and he thought in his heart: How shall I go in peace and without sorrow? Nay, not without a wound in the spirit shall I leave this city.

Long were the days of pain I have spent within its walls, and long were the nights of aloneness; and who can depart from his pain and his aloneness without regret?

我曾把太多的心靈片段散落於街道上,並且曾經多麼渴望孩子們打赤腳走在這些山丘上,而我無法不帶任何負擔和疼痛而離去。

今日,我不是脫去一件外衣,而是用自己的手撕開一層外皮。我留在身後的不是一個念頭,而是一顆渴望且甜蜜的心。

但我將不會在此逗留了。

召喚萬物的大海已在呼喚著我,我必須登船離去。時間在深夜仍如火炙燃燒,留下則意味著會被冰凍,被凝結成塊。

我很想帶走這裡的一切,但我怎麼能夠?

唇舌賦予聲音飛翔的翅膀,而聲音只能獨自翱翔天際。唯有老鷹不攜家帶眷而獨自飛翔,才能飛越太陽。

當他抵達山腳,再次面向大海時,他看到了船隻已駛近港灣,船頭上正站著來自家鄉的水手。

Too many fragments of the spirit have I scattered in these streets, and too many are the children of my longing that walk naked among these hills, and I cannot withdraw from them without a burden and an ache.

It is not a garment I cast off this day, but a skin that I tear with my own hands. Nor is it a thought I leave behind me, but a heart made sweet with hunger and with thirst.

Yet I cannot tarry longer. The sea that calls all things unto her calls me, and I must embark. For to stay, though the hours burn in the night, is to freeze and crystallize and be bound in a mould.

Fain would I take with me all that is here. But how shall I?

A voice cannot carry the tongue and the lips that give it wings. Alone must it seek the ether.

And alone and without his nest shall the eagle fly across the sun.

Now when he reached the foot of the hill, he turned again towards the sea, and he saw his ship approaching the harbour, and upon her prow the mariners, the men of his own land.

於是他的靈魂向他們大聲哭喊著說：

我古老母親的子孫們，你們乘著潮汐而來，

多少次你們航行在我的夢中。如今你們駛入我那更深的夢境，喚醒了我。

我已整裝待發，而今我的渴望揚起了帆，一起等待風起。

我只想在這平靜的空氣再呼一口氣，再回頭投以熱愛的一瞥。

然後我就會站到你們中間，就像一個航海者站在許多航海者之間。

而你，浩瀚的大海，這位不眠的母親，獨自帶給河流與小溪，所有的和平與自由，

只要等到溪流再繞過一道彎，林間空地再傳來一陣低語，我就將投進你的懷抱，正如同無窮之水滴融進無邊無際的大海當中。

And his soul cried out to them, and he said:

Sons of my ancient mother, you riders of the tides,

How often have you sailed in my dreams. And now you come in my awakening, which is my deeper dream.

Ready am I to go, and my eagerness with sails full set awaits the wind.

Only another breath will I breathe in this still air, only another loving look cast backward,

Then I shall stand among you, a seafarer among seafarers.

And you, vast sea, sleepless mother, Who alone are peace and freedom to the river and the stream,

Only another winding will this stream make, only another murmur in this glade, And then shall I come to you, a boundless drop to a boundless ocean.

行走間,他遙見男男女女們紛紛離開了農田與葡萄莊園,匆忙地走向城門去。

他聽到人們在呼喊著他的名字,在阡陌間互相大喊,通知船隻到來的消息。

他問自己:

難道分離的日子即是相聚的日子?

難道我的夜晚就是我的黎明?

我能為那些放下犁田農事、或是停止釀酒輪子的人們奉獻什麼呢?

是該將我的心靈化為一棵結實纍纍的樹,摘下果實與他們分享?

還是將我的渴望化作噴泉,對滿他們的酒杯?

我該化身為一座豎琴,任由強者之手用來撥彈,或是一管長笛,任由他的呼吸穿越我的身軀?

And as he walked he saw from afar men and women leaving their fields and their vineyards and hastening towards the city gates.

And he heard their voices calling his name, and shouting from field to field telling one another of the coming of the ship.

And he said to himself:

Shall the day of parting be the day of gathering?

And shall it be said that my eve was in truth my dawn?

And what shall I give unto him who has left his plough in midfurrow, or to him who has stopped the wheel of his winepress?

Shall my heart become a tree heavy-laden with fruit that I may gather and give unto them?

And shall my desires flow like a fountain that I may fill their cups?

Am I a harp that the hand of the mighty may touch me, or a flute that his breath may pass through me?

我是一個寂靜的尋求者，在寂靜中，我到底找得了什麼寶藏，可以放心地布施呢？

假如今日是我的收成之日，試問我是在何時何地撒下了種子呢？

假如此刻的確是我舉起燈籠之際，那燈中的焰火必然不屬於我。

我舉起的燈是空虛而黑暗的，夜的守護者將為它添滿油，並且點亮它。

他用言語訴說了這些，但還有更多話藏在心中未說出口。對他自己而言，他無法說出內心深處的秘密。

當他進入城中，人們都前來迎接，紛紛不約而同地呼喊著他。

城中的老者趨前說道：

請別就這樣離開。

你一直是我們黑暗中的黎明，你的青春給了我們美夢的希望。

A seeker of silences am I, and what treasure have I found in silences that I may dispense with confidence?

If this is my day of harvest, in what fields have I sowed the seed, and in what unrembered seasons?

If this indeed be the our in which I lift up my lantern, it is not my flame that shall burn therein.

Empty and dark shall I raise my lantern,

And the guardian of the night shall fill it with oil and he shall light it also.

These things he said in words. But much in his heart remained unsaid. For he himself could not speak his deeper secret.

And when he entered into the city all the people came to meet him, and they were crying out to him as with one voice.

And the elders of the city stood forth and said:

Go not yet away from us.

A noontide have you been in our twilight, and your youth has given us dreams to dream.

在我們之間,你既不是陌生者,也不是客人,你是我們的兒子、我們心愛的人。不要讓我們因渴望見到你的面容,而使眼睛忍受苦楚。

男女祭司對他說:

如今,請不要讓海洋的波浪阻隔了我們,不要讓我們共度的歲月成為追憶。

你曾像一個精靈似的,行走在我們之間,你的影子像光輝般,投映在我們的臉龐。

我們是如此地愛著你。卻未曾將我們對你的愛說出口,像是被層層面紗所掩蓋。如今大聲地呼喚你,在你面前推誠布公。

直到分隔兩地時,才知道愛有多深。

其他人也走上前向他表達慰留之意。

但他沒有回答,只是低著頭,身旁的人看到他的淚水滴落在胸襟。

No stranger are you among us, nor a guest, but our son and our dearly beloved. Suffer not yet our eyes to hunger for your face.

And the priests and the priestesses said unto him:

Let not the waves of the sea separate us now, and the years you have spent in our midst become a memory.

You have walked among us a spirit, and your shadow has been a light upon our faces.

Much have we loved you. But speechless was our love, and with veils has it been veiled. Yet now it cries aloud unto you, and would stand revealed before you.

And ever has it been that love knows not its own depth until the hour of separation.

And others came also and entreated him.

But he answered them not. He only bent his head; and those who stood near saw his tears falling upon his breast.

他與人們一起走向神殿前的大廣場。一位名叫阿蜜翠的女子迎出神殿。她是一位女預言家。

他非常溫柔地注視著她，因為她正是在他到達這座城市的第一天就追隨他，信奉他的那位。

她向他致賀並說道：

上帝的先知，為了追尋極致，你長久以來一直在搜尋著那條航行的路，

如今船隻已到，你必定會離開了。

你是如此地深切渴望著那記憶中的土地，如此希冀那偉大的夢想所在；我們的愛不會約束著你，我們的需要也不會控制住你。

不過，請你在離開之前，向我們談談，為我們說說你的真理。我們將把它傳給我們的子女，他們再傳給他們的子孫，使真理永不消滅。

And he and the people proceeded towards the great square before the temple. And there came out of the sanctuary a woman whose name was Almitra. And she was a seeress.

And he looked upon her with exceeding tenderness, for it was she who had first sought and believed in him when he had been but a day in their city.

And she hailed him, saying:

Prophet of God, in quest for the uttermost, long have you searched the distances for your ship.

And now your ship has come, and you must needs go.

Deep is your longing for the land of your memories and the dwelling place of your greater desires; and our love would not bind you nor our needs hold you.

Yet this we ask ere you leave us, that you speak to us and give us of your truth. And we will give it unto our children, and they unto their children, and it shall not perish.

在你的孤獨中，你曾看顧過我們的白天，在你清醒中，你曾聆聽過我們睡夢中的哭泣與歡笑。

現在請揭曉我們自身的所有，告訴我們，你所知道的一切關於生與死的問題。

他回答道：

阿法利斯城的民眾啊，我此刻除了要說些感動你們靈魂中的事物之外，還能說些什麼呢！

In your aloneness you have watched with our days, and in your wakefulness you have listened to the weeping and the laughter of our sleep.

Now therefore disclose us to ourselves, and tell us all that has been shown you of that which is between birth and death.

And he answered,

People of Orphalese, of what can I speak save of that which is even now moving your souls?

02 關於愛

於是阿蜜翠說，請為我們談談愛吧。

他抬頭看著人群，眾人此刻一片安靜。接著他以洪亮的聲音說：

當愛揮手向你們召喚時，就跟著它走吧，儘管他的道路既艱難又驚險。

當他的展開雙翼擁抱你們時，就投入他的懷抱吧，儘管藏在他翅膀中的利刃會刺傷你們。

當他對你們說話時，相信他吧，儘管他的聲音可能會粉碎你的夢，如同北風狂掃花園中的花朵。

就像愛在為你們加冕之時，也同時會將你們釘上十字架。

即使他可助你們成長向上，也能將你們削剪向下。

即便他會攀上你們的高處，撫摸你們在陽光下顫動的嫩枝，

但他也會向下延伸並動搖緊附在大地上的樹根。

02
On Love

Then said Almitra, "Speak to us of Love."

And he raised his head and looked upon the people, and there fell a stillness upon them. And with a great voice he said:

When love beckons to you follow him, Though his ways are hard and steep.

And when his wings enfold you yield to him, Though the sword hidden among his pinions may wound you.

And when he speaks to you believe in him, Though his voice may shatter your dreams as the north wind lays waste the garden.

For even as love crowns you so shall he crucify you..

Even as he is for your growth so is he for your pruning.

Even as he ascends to your height and caresses your tenderest branches that quiver in the sun,

So shall he descend to your roots and shake them in their clinging to the earth.

愛把你們像一束穀物般，捆綁在他的身邊。

他把你們脫去了稻穀，使你們赤裸。

他把你們篩選過後，使你們脫去穀糠。

他把你們反覆碾磨，直至潔白。

他把你們捏製揉合，直至彈滑柔順。

然後，他把你們放在聖火上，讓你們能成為上帝饗宴上的聖餅。

這一切都是愛為你們所做，使你們能從中領悟自己心中的秘密，使這種認知成為生命本質的一小部分。

但若因為畏懼，只知尋求愛的和平與愛的快樂，

那麼你們還不如遮掩自己的赤裸，退出愛的打穀場，

進到那無季節變化的世界，在那裡，你應會開懷，卻無法盡情歡笑；

你應會哭泣，卻無法流乾淚水。

愛除了自身，別無所予亦無所求。

愛不該佔有亦不該被佔有；愛有了自身便已足夠。

Like sheaves of corn he gathers you unto himself.

He threshes you to make you naked.

He sifts you to free you from your husks.

He grinds you to whiteness.

He kneads you until you are pliant;

And then he assigns you to his sacred fire, that you may become sacred bread for God's sacred feast.

All these things shall love do unto you that you may know the secrets of your heart, and in that knowledge become a fragment of Life's heart.

But if in your fear you would seek only love's peace and love's pleasure,

Then it is better for you that you cover your nakedness and pass out of love's threshing-floor,

Into the seasonless world where you shall laugh, but not all of your laughter, and weep, but not all of your tears.

Love gives naught but itself and takes naught but from itself.

Love possesses not nor would it be possessed; For love is sufficient unto love.

當你付出了愛，你不該說：「上帝在我心中」，而是說：「我在上帝心中」。

別以為你可以左右愛的方向，如果愛認為你值得的話，則會為你指引方向。

愛別無他求，只求成全愛的本身。

但如果你愛了，又偏偏有所求，那麼就讓這些成為所求吧：

讓自身融化為一道奔流的小溪，在夜晚歌唱出他的旋律。

去體會過多的溫柔帶來的痛苦。

被自己對愛的領悟所傷害。

即使流血，也死心塌地。

在黎明，帶著一顆飛行的心醒來，感謝又一個充滿愛的日子；

在午休，一邊休息、一邊冥想著愛的醉人；

在黃昏，帶著感恩的心返家；

在睡前，為你心中的摯愛祈禱，在唇間吟誦讚美的詩歌。

When you love you should not say, "God is in my heart," but rather, I am in the heart of God."

And think not you can direct the course of love, if it finds you worthy, directs your course.

Love has no other desire but to fulfill itself.

But if you love and must needs have desires, let these be your desires:

To melt and be like a running brook that sings its melody to the night.

To know the pain of too much tenderness.

To be wounded by your own understanding of love;

And to bleed willingly and joyfully.

To wake at dawn with a winged heart and give thanks for another day of loving;

To rest at the noon hour and meditate love's ecstasy;

To return home at eventide with gratitude;

And then to sleep with a prayer for the beloved in your heart and a song of praise upon your lips.

關於婚姻

接著，阿蜜翠又開口問道：「那麼婚姻呢，大師？」

他回答道：

你們同時出生，你們必將永遠相依偎。

即便到了死神的白色羽翼分散你們的日子，你們也將形影不離。

啊，即使在上帝無聲的回憶裡，你們仍將在一起。

但在彼此相愛，但不要使愛變成束縛；

好讓天堂之風在你們之間飛舞。

彼此相愛，但不要使愛變成束縛；

讓愛成為你們靈魂之岸間的奔流大海。

斟滿彼此的酒杯，但不要只飲同一杯。

分享彼此的麵包，但不要只吃同一條麵包。

03
On Marriage

Then Almitra spoke again and said, "And what of Marriage, master?"

And he answered saying:

You were born together, and together you shall be forevermore.

You shall be together when white wings of death scatter your days.

Aye, you shall be together even in the silent memory of God.

But let there be spaces in your togetherness,

And let the winds of the heavens dance between you.

Love one another but make not a bond of love:

Let it rather be a moving sea between the shores of your souls.

Fill each other's cup but drink not from one cup.

Give one another of your bread but eat not from the same loaf.

一同歡樂地載歌載舞，但要彼此保持獨立，

琵琶的琴弦也彼此分開，即使它們同彈奏一首樂曲。

奉獻你們的心，但無需讓對方保管。

因為唯有生命之手才能容納你們的心。

你們要站在一起，但不要太過於靠近；

即便是神殿的支柱，也是分開聳立的，

還有橡樹和柏樹，也無法在彼此的蔭影下生長。

Sing and dance together and be joyous, but let each one of you be alone,

Even as the strings of a lute are alone though they quiver with the same music.

Give your hearts, but not into each other's keeping.

For only the hand of Life can contain your hearts.

And stand together, yet not too near together:

For the pillars of the temple stand apart,

And the oak tree and the cypress grow not in each other's shadow.

關於孩子

一位懷抱嬰兒的婦女說：「請跟我們談談孩子吧。」

他說道：

你們的孩子並不是你們的孩子。

他們是渴求擁有自我生命的子女。

他們經你們而來，卻非來自於你們。

儘管他們跟你們在一起，但並不屬於你們。

你可以給他們的，是你的愛而非想法，

因為他們有自己的想法。

你們可以建房給他們的身體居住，但無法讓他們的靈魂居住在裡面，

因為他們的靈魂住在明日之屋中，即使在夢中你們也無法探訪。

你們可以努力模仿他們，但不可以試圖要他們像你們一樣。

因為生命無法倒退，也不會逗留於昨日。

04
On Children

And a woman who held a babe against her bosom said, "Speak to us of Children."

And he said:

Your children are not your children.

They are the sons and daughters of Life's longing for itself.

They come through you but not from you,

And though they are with you, yet they belong not to you.

You may give them your love but not your thoughts.

For they have their own thoughts.

You may house their bodies but not their souls,

For their souls dwell in the house of tomorrow, which you cannot visit, not even in your dreams.

You may strive to be like them, but seek not to make them like you.

For life goes not backward nor tarries with yesterday.

如果你們是弓,那麼你們的孩子便是被發射出的活躍之箭。

弓箭手看準在永恆小徑上的箭靶,施展全力將你拉開,使箭射得又快又遠。

愉悅地在弓箭手的手中彎曲吧;

因為他既愛那飛馳的箭,也愛那平穩的弓。

You are the bows from which your children as living arrows are sent forth.

The archer sees the mark upon the path of the infinite, and He bends you with His might that His arrows may go swift and far.

Let your bending in the archer's hand be for gladness;

For even as he loves the arrow that flies, so He loves also the bow that is stable.

關於施予

接著一位富人說：「請為我們談談施予。」

他回答：

當你們施捨財物時，這樣的施予是非常微小的。

當你們奉獻自己時，才是真正的施予。

因為你們的財產不就是一些你們擔心明天可能需要用到，因此去保有、去維護的東西嗎？

謹慎的小狗，在追隨朝聖者去聖城前，把骨頭先埋藏在荒沙裡，但明天，明天又能給牠帶來什麼呢？

對需求的恐懼，不就是需求本身嗎？

當你們的井水已經滿溢，但仍害怕會口渴，這個渴望豈不是永無止盡嗎？

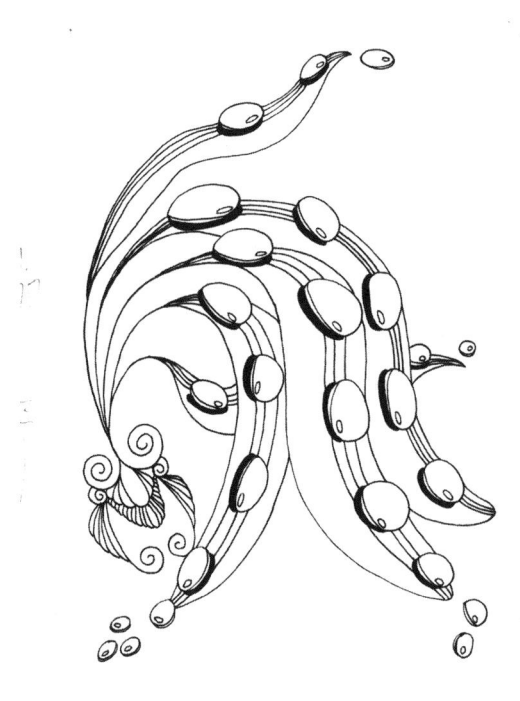

On Giving

Then said a rich man, "Speak to us of Giving."

And he answered:

You give but little when you give of your possessions.

It is when you give of yourself that you truly give.

For what are your possessions but things you keep and guard for fear you may need them tomorrow?

And tomorrow, what shall tomorrow bring to the overprudent dog burying bones in the trackless sand as he follows the pilgrims to the holy city?

And what is fear of need but need itself?

Is not dread of thirst when your well is full, thirst that is unquenchable?

有些人只捐贈自己擁有的少部份財產——他們只是為了獲得名聲，而他們所隱藏的欲望卻使得他們的饋贈變得一無是處。

也有一些人，他們擁有甚少，卻付出了全部。信仰者們都相信生命與生命的賜予，他們的儲蓄從不匱乏。

那些快樂的施予者，他們所獲得的回報就是快樂。

那些痛苦的施予者，他們所獲得的回報就是痛苦做為洗禮。

還有一些人，施予時並不感覺痛苦，也不是為了尋求快樂，或被人歌功頌德；

他們的施予，就像遠方山谷邊的桃金孃散發芳香。透過這些人手中，上帝在向大家布道，透過他們的雙眸，上帝在向大地微笑。

雖然被要求施予很好，但若能透過體諒，在別人提出要求之前相贈的話，這是更高的境界；

There are those who give little of the much which they have -- and they give it for recognition and their hidden desire makes their gifts unwholesome.

And there are those who have little and give it all.

These are the believers in life and the bounty of life, and their coffer is never empty.

There are those who give with joy, and that joy is their reward.

And there are those who give with pain, and that pain is their baptism.

And there are those who give and know not pain in giving, nor do they seek joy, nor give with mindfulness of virtue;

They give as in yonder valley the myrtle breathes its fragrance into space.

Though the hands of such as these God speaks, and from behind their eyes He smiles upon the earth.

It is well to give when asked, but it is better to give unasked, through understanding;

對於慷慨大方的人而言，施比受有福。

你們還有什麼要保留的呢？

你所有的一切，終究有一天都將施予他人；

所以從今天起就施予吧，奉獻的時機由你自己決定，而不是由你的繼承人來決定。

你們常說：「我只為值得的人施予。」

但你們果園中的樹木可不是這樣說的，你牧場上的羊群也不會這樣說。

它們奉獻因而得到生存，而保留意味著滅亡。

一個值得擁有白晝與黑夜的人，當然也值得從你們這裡獲得其他的一切。

一個值得從生命之海裡飄飲的人，當然也值得用你們的小溪斟滿水杯。

And to the open-handed the search for one who shall receive is joy greater than giving.

And is there aught you would withhold?

All you have shall some day be given;

Therefore give now, that the season of giving may be yours and not your inheritors'.

You often say, "I would give, but only to the deserving."

The trees in your orchard say not so, nor the flocks in your pasture.

They give that they may live, for to withhold is to perish.

Surely he who is worthy to receive his days and his nights is worthy of all else from you.

And he who has deserved to drink from the ocean of life deserves to fill his cup from your little stream.

還有什麼比那能夠接受施捨的勇氣、信心更值得施予的呢？

你又是誰？人們就得為你剖開胸膛，露出他們的自尊，讓你看到他們赤裸的價值和無袱的尊嚴嗎？

先看看自己是否配作一個施予者，一個施予的工具。

事實是，是生命給予了生命——而你，自以為自己是施予者，其實只是一個見證者罷了。

至於你們這些受到施予的人——你們的確都是受施者——母須承著感恩的負擔，以免給你自己和施予者都套上束縛。

不如藉著施予者的施予，如同借著翅膀一樣，一起飛上天空吧，

如果一直耿耿於懷你所欠的，就表示你懷疑了那位寬大為懷的大地為母，上帝為父的施予者對你的慷慨了。

And what desert greater shall there be than that which lies in the courage and the confidence, nay the charity, of receiving?

And who are you that men should rend their bosom and unveil their pride, that you may see their worth naked and their pride unabashed?

See first that you yourself deserve to be a giver, and an instrument of giving.

For in truth it is life that gives unto life -- while you, who deem yourself a giver, are but a witness.

And you receivers -- and you are all receivers -- assume no weight of gratitude, lest you lay a yoke upon yourself and upon him who gives.

Rather rise together with the giver on his gifts as on wings;

For to be overmindful of your debt, is to doubt his generosity who has the free-hearted earth for mother, and God for father.

06 關於飲食

然後一位老人，旅館的主人說道：「請給我們談談飲食吧。」

他說道：

雖然希望你們能靠大地的芬芳生存，如同氣生植物靠陽光維持生命。

但既然你們必須殺生為食，還要從羔羊口中搶奪它們的母乳以解渴，那姑且把這個行為當做一種崇敬方式吧。

在你們的膳食上立起一座祭壇，紀念森林與平原裡的那些純潔、天真，是為了更加更加的純真而犧牲。

當你們宰殺一隻禽畜，你們應在心中對它說：

「現在屠宰你的力量也將屠宰我，同樣我也會被吞食、被屠宰。把你送到我手中的這條法則，也將把我送到更強者的手中。

你同我的血，都只是滋養天國之樹的汁液。」

On Eating And Drinking

Then an old man, a keeper of an inn, said, "Speak to us of Eating and Drinking."

And he said:

Would that you could live on the fragrance of the earth, and like an air plant be sustained by the light.

But since you must kill to eat, and rob the young of its mother's milk to quench your thirst, let it then be an act of worship,

And let your board stand an altar on which the pure and the innocent of forest and plain are sacrificed for that which is purer and still more innocent in many.

When you kill a beast say to him in your heart,

"By the same power that slays you, I to am slain; and I too shall be consumed.

For the law that delivered you into my hand shall deliver me into a mightier hand.

Your blood and my blood is naught but the sap that feeds the tree of heaven."

當你們用牙咀嚼一個蘋果時，你們應在心中對它說：

「你的種子將種植在我的體內，你明日的芽苞將在我心中結果，你的芬芳將融入我的氣息，你我將共同慶賀所有的季節。」

在秋季，當你們採集葡萄園中釀製紅酒時，請在你們的心中說：

「我是一座葡萄園，我的果實也將被採集榨汁釀酒，我就像新酒一般，將被保存在永恆的容器裡。」

在冬季，當你們汲酒而飲時，請在心中為每一杯酒唱上一曲吧；讓歌聲憶起秋日、葡萄園和酒莊釀製的時刻。

And when you crush an apple with your teeth, say to it in your heart,

"Your seeds shall live in my body, And the buds of your tomorrow shall blossom in my heart,

And your fragrance shall be my breath, And together we shall rejoice through all the seasons.'

And in the autumn, when you gather the grapes of your vineyard for the winepress, say in you heart,

"I to am a vineyard, and my fruit shall be gathered for the winepress, And like new wine I shall be kept in eternal vessels."

And in winter, when you draw the wine, let there be in your heart a song for each cup;

And let there be in the song a remembrance for the autumn days, and for the vineyard, and for the winepress.

關於工作

一位農夫說，「請為我們談談工作。」

他答道：

你們工作，才能夠與大地和大地的靈魂並駕齊驅。

你們若偷懶，就會變為季節的陌生人，落後於生命的行列，不再帶著莊嚴和自豪的順從邁向永恆的行列。

當你工作時，就像是一支蘆笛，時間的耳語會透過你的心化作音樂。

當你們所有人都齊聲合唱時，誰願意做一根沉默無聲的蘆葦？

一直以來，總有人告訴你們：工作如同是詛咒，勞動如同是不幸。

但我要對你們說：當你們工作時，就是實現了土地夢想最深刻的一部份，在夢想成形時，這部分便已指派給你。

你們保持勞動，才是真實地熱愛生命，

透過勞動去熱愛生命，就是與生命最深的秘密做了親密的結合。

On Work

Then a ploughman said, "Speak to us of Work."

And he answered, saying:

You work that you may keep pace with the earth and the soul of the earth.

For to be idle is to become a stranger unto the seasons, and to step out of life's procession, that marches in majesty and proud submission towards the infinite.

When you work you are a flute through whose heart the whispering of the hours turns to music.

Which of you would be a reed, dumb and silent, when all else sings together in unison?

Always you have been told that work is a curse and labour a misfortune.

But I say to you that when you work you fulfil a part of earth's furthest dream, assigned to you when that dream was born,

And in keeping yourself with labour you are in truth loving life,

And to love life through labour is to be intimate with life's inmost secret.

然而，如果你們在努力中，視出生為苦難，視維持肉體生存當成寫在額頭上的詛咒，那麼我要告訴你們，只有辛苦勞動流下額頭上的汗水，才能洗去那些字跡。

人們總對你們說人生是黑暗的，當你感到疲倦時，更會重複著這句疲憊話語。

但我說，人生的確是黑暗的，直到有了驅動力，
所有驅動力都是盲目的，直到有了知識，
一切知識都是徒勞，除非有充實的工作，
所有工作淪為空談，除非把愛傾入其中；
當你們帶著愛去工作時，你們就與自己、與他人、與上帝互為一體。

什麼是帶著愛去工作？
從你心中的針線來縫織，彷彿你心愛的人將穿上這衣服。

But if you in your pain call birth an affliction and the support of the flesh a curse written upon your brow, then I answer that naught but the sweat of your brow shall wash away that which is written.

You have been told also life is darkness, and in your weariness you echo what was said by the weary.

And I say that life is indeed darkness save when there is urge,

And all urge is blind save when there is knowledge,

And all knowledge is vain save when there is work,

And all work is empty save when there is love;

And when you work with love you bind yourself to yourself, and to one another, and to God.

And what is it to work with love?

It is to weave the cloth with threads drawn from your heart, even as if your beloved were to wear that cloth.

用感情來建造房子，彷彿你心愛的人將居住其中。

用溫柔來播種，帶著喜悅來收割，彷彿你心愛的人將品嘗果實。

用自己心靈的氣息去改變一切事物。

並且去了解到所有受福的逝者都在身邊注視著你。

我曾經聽見你們說，彷彿在夢中呢喃道：「在大理石中埋首工作，在石頭中找到自己心靈形象的人，比耕地者更加高貴。

捕捉彩虹，並且將它彩繪在畫布上的人，更勝於幫我們製作草鞋的人。」

但是我要說──不是在睡夢中，而是在格外清醒的日正當中，當風對著巨大橡樹說話時，並不如對著片片青葉說話時來得溫柔，

藉由自己的愛，把風聲變為歌聲，使之更加甜美，他才是偉大的。

It is to build a house with affection, even as if your beloved were to dwell in that house.

It is to sow seeds with tenderness and reap the harvest with joy, even as if your beloved were to eat the fruit.

It is to charge all things you fashion with a breath of your own spirit,

And to know that all the blessed dead are standing about you and watching.

Often have I heard you say, as if speaking in sleep, "he who works in marble, and finds the shape of his own soul in the stone, is a nobler than he who ploughs the soil.

And he who seizes the rainbow to lay it on a cloth in the likeness of man, is more than he who makes the sandals for our feet."

But I say, not in sleep but in the over--wakefulness of noontide, that the wind speaks not more sweetly to the giant oaks than to the least of all the blades of grass;

And he alone is great who turns the voice of the wind into a song made sweeter by his own loving.

工作就是把愛化為有形。

假如你們無法帶著愛去工作，只是一味覺得厭惡，那麼你們不如放棄工作，坐在殿宇門前，等待那些以工作為樂的人們給你們施捨。

如果你們只是漫不經心地去烘焙麵包，那麼你們烤出的麵包將會變苦，預多讓人半飽。

假如你們心不甘情不願地搾葡萄，那麼你們的怨恨就會變成毒液，滲入酒中。

即使你們歌唱如天使一般，若不熱愛歌唱，那麼你們仍將搗住人們的耳朵，讓他們聽不見日夜之聲。

Work is love made visible.

And if you cannot work with love but only with distaste, it is better that you should leave your work and sit at the gate of the temple and take alms of those who work with joy.

For if you bake bread with indifference, you bake a bitter bread that feeds but half man's hunger.

And if you grudge the crushing of the grapes, your grudge distils a poison in the wine.

And if you sing though as angels, and love not the singing, you muffle man's ears to the voices of the day and the voices of the night.

08 關於歡樂與憂愁

一位女子說：「請給我們講講歡樂和憂愁。」

他答道：

你們的歡樂就是撕下面具的憂愁。

你的笑聲常常和滿臉的淚水一同湧出。

不然是怎麼樣呢？

悲哀刻劃在你們身上越深，你們就能包容越多的喜樂。

不就是支曾經受過陶藝家的爐火中燒製而成的酒杯，如今拿來斟滿你們的葡萄美酒？

不就是那棵曾經被刀子掏空的樹木，如今成為撫慰你們心靈的琵琶？

當你們在歡樂之際，請深深地反省自己的心靈，就會發現如今帶給你們歡樂的，正是曾經帶給你們憂愁的。

On Joy And Sorrow

Then a woman said, "Speak to us of Joy and Sorrow."

And he answered:

Your joy is your sorrow unmasked.

And the selfsame well from which your laughter rises was oftentimes filled with your tears.

And how else can it be?

The deeper that sorrow carves into your being, the more joy you can contain.

Is not the cup that hold your wine the very cup that was burned in the potter's oven?

And is not the lute that soothes your spirit, the very wood that was hollowed with knives?

When you are joyous, look deep into your heart and you shall find it is only that which has given you sorrow that is giving you joy.

當你們感到悲哀之時,請審視自己的心靈,也會發現事實上,今日帶給你們憂愁的,正是曾經帶給你們歡樂的。

你們其中一些人說:「欣喜更甚於悲傷。」而另一些人說:「不,憂愁甚於歡樂。」

但我對你們說,它們是密不可分的。

它們一同來臨,當其中一個獨自與你坐在餐席上時,要記得另一個正在你的床上安眠。

的確,你們就像是天秤一樣,搖擺於憂愁與歡樂之間。

只有當你們完全平靜時,才會保持靜止與平衡。

當寶藏守護者把你高高舉起來秤量他的金銀財寶時,你的歡樂和憂愁便會為之起起伏伏了。

When you are sorrowful look again in your heart, and you shall see that in truth you are weeping for that which has been your delight.

Some of you say, "Joy is greater than sorrow," and others say, "Nay, sorrow is the greater."

But I say unto you, they are inseparable.

Together they come, and when one sits alone with you at your board, remember that the other is asleep upon your bed.

Verily you are suspended like scales between your sorrow and your joy.

Only when you are empty are you at standstill and balanced.

When the treasure-keeper lifts you to weigh his gold and his silver, needs must your joy or your sorrow rise or fall.

關於房子

接著一位泥水匠上前說道：「請給我們談談房子吧。」

他答道：

你們在城牆內建造房屋之前，請先運用想像力，假設在荒野裡建了一座涼亭。

正如同當夜暮低垂時，你們有家可歸，你們心中遙遠而孤單的流浪者們也是這麼想著。

房子就是你們更大的身軀。

它在陽光底下生長，在寂靜的夜裡成眠，這不是做夢。難道你們的房子都沒有夢嗎？沒有做過想遠離城市，前往樹林中或山上的夢嗎？

我願將你們的房舍聚集在手中，像一位播種者把它們撒向森林和草地。

On Houses

Then a mason came forth and said, "Speak to us of Houses."

And he answered and said:

Build of your imaginings a bower in the wilderness ere you build a house within the city walls.

For even as you have home-comings in your twilight, so has the wanderer in you, the ever distant and alone.

Your house is your larger body.

It grows in the sun and sleeps in the stillness of the night; and it is not dreamless. Does not your house dream? And dreaming, leave the city for grove or hilltop?

Would that I could gather your houses into my hand, and like a sower scatter them in forest and meadow.

願山谷就是你們的街道，綠徑就是你們的小巷，那麼你們便可以穿過葡萄園拜訪彼此，你的外衣還留著土壤的芬芳。

然而，這些夢想卻還無法成真。

由於你們的祖先生活在恐懼中，所以把大家聚集靠攏一起。這個恐懼一時之間不會散去，你們住家爐灶和田地會被城牆分隔一段時間。

阿法利斯城的人們，告訴我，你們的房屋中有些什麼？你們用緊閉的門守護什麼呢？

你們可曾擁有平靜，去激發力量中沉靜的驅動力？

你們可曾擁有回憶，那座跨越心靈最高峰的閃亮拱橋？

你們可曾擁有美好，把心從成型木石引導到聖山？

告訴我，你們的房屋可擁有這些？

Would the valleys were your streets, and the green paths your alleys, that you might seek one another through vineyards, and come with the fragrance of the earth in your garments.

But these things are not yet to be.

In their fear your forefathers gathered you too near together. And that fear shall endure a little longer. A little longer shall your city walls separate your hearths from your fields.

And tell me, people of Orphalese, what have you in these houses? And what is it you guard with fastened doors?

Have you peace, the quiet urge that reveals your power?

Have you remembrances, the glimmering arches that span the summits of the mind?

Have you beauty, that leads the heart from things fashioned of wood and stone to the holy mountain?

Tell me, have you these in your houses?

或者你只有安逸和追求安逸的欲望——這東西鬼祟地入室，並且反客為主，進而成為主人翁？

唉，它竟化作一名馴獸師，用誘餌和鞭子來做成你們更大欲望的玩偶。

它的手儘管柔軟如絲，但它的心卻硬如鋼鐵。

它站在床邊催人入睡，並對於健全的感官嗤之以鼻。它嘲笑你們的聽覺，把它們塞放在薊做的毛絨裡，如同易碎的器皿。

的確，貪圖安逸的欲望謀殺了靈魂的熱情，而它還在葬禮上獰笑著。

但身為蒼穹大地的兒女們，即使在休息之中，你們的心靈也不要落入陷阱或被馴服。

你們的居室不應是錨，而應是桅杆。

它不應當是用來遮掩傷口的閃耀薄皮，而應是用來保護眼睛的眼皮。

Or have you only comfort, and the lust for comfort, that stealthy thing that enters the house a guest, and becomes a host, and then a master?

Ay, and it becomes a tamer, and with hook and scourge makes puppets of your larger desires.

Though its hands are silken, its heart is of iron.

It lulls you to sleep only to stand by your bed and jeer at the dignity of the flesh. It makes mock of your sound senses, and lays them in thistledown like fragile vessels.

Verily the lust for comfort murders the passion of the soul, and then walks grinning in the funeral.

But you, children of space, you restless in rest, you shall not be trapped nor tamed.

Your house shall be not an anchor but a mast.

It shall not be a glistening film that covers a wound, but an eyelid that guards the eye.

你們不應為了穿過房門而收起雙翼，不應為防止撞到天花板而彎腰低頭，也不應因唯恐牆壁坍塌而不敢呼吸。

你們不應居住在死人為生人築造的墳墓中。

無論你們的住所是如何地碧綠輝煌，但它們也不應當隱藏你們的秘密，掩蓋你們的渴望。

因為在你們內心無窮盡的願望就是居住於碧空之殿，晨霧是它的門，夜晚是它的歌聲，寂靜是它的窗。

You shall not fold your wings that you may pass through doors, nor bend your heads that they strike not against a ceiling, nor fear to breathe lest walls should crack and fall down.

You shall not dwell in tombs made by the dead for the living.

And though of magnificence and splendour, your house shall not hold your secret nor shelter your longing.

For that which is boundless in you abides in the mansion of the sky, whose door is the morning mist, and whose windows are the songs and the silences of night.

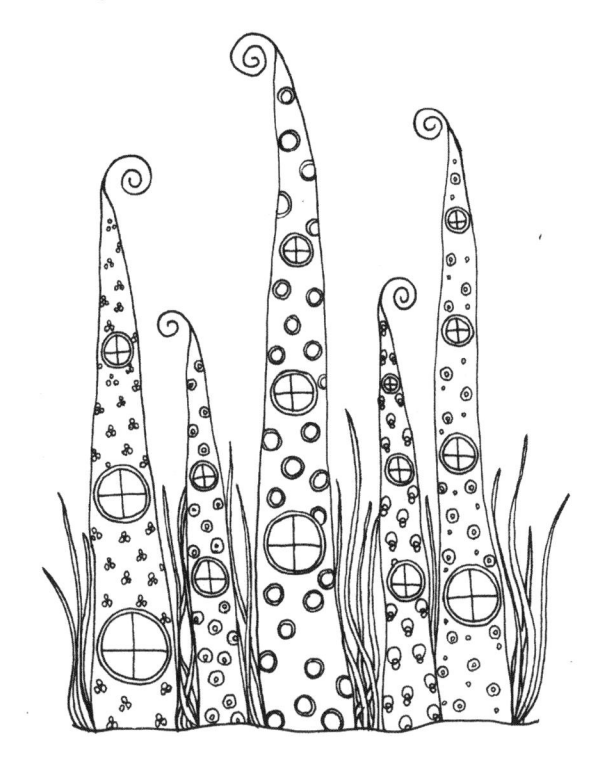

10 關於衣服

一位織工說：「請給我們談談衣服。」

他答道：

你們的衣服遮掩了你們許多的美，卻遮蓋不住醜陋。

雖然你們想借由衣服追求隱私的自由，但卻有可能在當中找到的卻是鞚具和鎖鏈。

但願你們用自己的肌膚而不是用衣服去迎接陽光和微風，因為陽光中有生命的氣息，而微風中有生命之手。

你們有些人說：「是北風使我們編織了所穿的衣服。」

我說沒錯，的確是北風。

但北風是把羞怯做為織布機，把纖弱的身體做為針線。

當北風完成工作時，便會在林中大笑。

On Clothes

And the weaver said, "Speak to us of Clothes."

And he answered:

Your clothes conceal much of your beauty, yet they hide not the unbeautiful.

And though you seek in garments the freedom of privacy you may find in them a harness and a chain.

Would that you could meet the sun and the wind with more of your skin and less of your raiment,

For the breath of life is in the sunlight and the hand of life is in the wind.

Some of you say, "It is the north wind who has woven the clothes to wear."

And I say, Aye, it was the north wind,

But shame was his loom, and the softening of the sinews was his thread.

And when his work was done he laughed in the forest.

別忘了,羞怯是用來抵擋邪狎的盾牌。

若沒有任何邪狎,那羞怯除了是心靈上的束縛和腐敗外,還能是什麼?

也不要忘記,大地非常喜歡去感受你的赤足,風兒非常渴望玩弄你的頭髮。

Forget not that modesty is for a shield against the eye of the unclean.

And when the unclean shall be no more, what were modesty but a fetter and a fouling of the mind?

And forget not that the earth delights to feel your bare feet and the winds long to play with your hair.

關於買賣

11

一位商人說:「請給我們談談買賣。」

他回答道:

大地將果實賜予你們,如果你們不知要如何盛在手上,就不應該伸手去捧著它們。

你們應當在交換大地的禮物中,感到富裕與滿足。

但除非此種交換是在愛與友善的公平中進行,否則便會引起一些人的貪念,另一些人卻感到飢渴。

當你們這些在海上、田間和果園裡工作的勞動者們,與織工、陶匠和採集香料的人們在市場上相遇時,

應要祈求大地的主神來到你們之中,讓祂使你們那核算價值的評量天秤變得神聖。

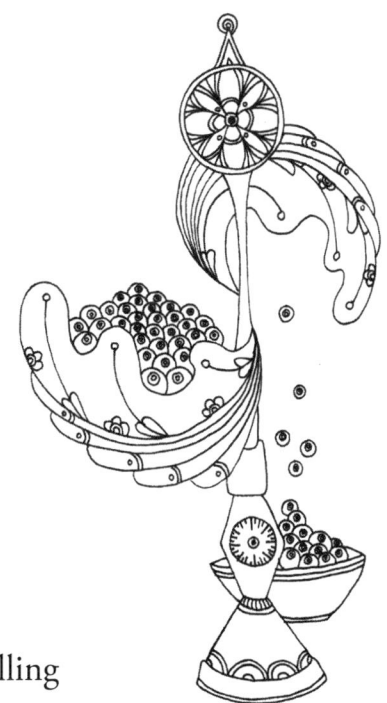

On Buying And Selling

And a merchant said, "Speak to us of Buying and Selling."

And he answered and said:

To you the earth yields her fruit, and you shall not want if you but know how to fill your hands.

It is in exchanging the gifts of the earth that you shall find abundance and be satisfied.

Yet unless the exchange be in love and kindly justice, it will but lead some to greed and others to hunger.

When in the market place you toilers of the sea and fields and vineyards meet the weavers and the potters and the gatherers of spices,

Invoke then the master spirit of the earth, to come into your midst and sanctify the scales and the reckoning that weighs value against value.

勿讓遊手好閒的人參與你們的買賣，他們會以言語來騙取你們的勞動。

你們應該對這些人說：

「咱們一同去耕田吧，和我們的兄弟一同去海上撒網吧；因為土地和海洋對你們就像對我們一樣慷慨大方。」

如果有演唱或跳舞、吹笛的人也來到市場，──你們也應當買下他們的禮物。

因為他們也採集了果實和乳香，而他們所帶來的，就像是用夢想打造出來，你們的的靈魂衣食。

在你們離開市集之前，審視一下是否有人空手而歸。

否則大地的主神不會安眠於風中，直到你們每人的需求都得到滿足。

And suffer not the barren-handed to take part in your transactions, who would sell their words for your labour.

To such men you should say,

"Come with us to the field, or go with our brothers to the sea and cast your net; For the land and the sea shall be bountiful to you even as to us."

And if there come the singers and the dancers and the flute players, -- buy of their gifts also.

For they too are gatherers of fruit and frankincense, and that which they bring, though fashioned of dreams, is raiment and food for your soul.

And before you leave the marketplace, see that no one has gone his way with empty hands.

For the master spirit of the earth shall not sleep peacefully upon the wind till the needs of the least of you are satisfied.

12 關於罪與罰

城中的一位法官上前說道:「請為我們講講罪與罰。」

他回答說:

當你們的心靈隨風徘徊之時,你們孤零而失慎地錯待別人,也就是對自己犯了過錯。

為了所犯下的過錯,在不受重視之下,你們必須去敲那受神眷顧之人的門,且必會受到冷落。

你們自我的神性就像大海;永遠保持純潔無瑕。

又像天空,幫助有翼者飛翔。

甚至你們自我的神性也像太陽;它既不知道老鼠的方位,也不會去尋找毒蛇的洞穴。

但你們自身並非只有神性存在。

On Crime And Punishment

Then one of the judges of the city stood forth and said, "Speak to us of Crime and Punishment."

And he answered saying:

It is when your spirit goes wandering upon the wind,

That you, alone and unguarded, commit a wrong unto others and therefore unto yourself.

And for that wrong committed must you knock and wait a while unheeded at the gate of the blessed.

Like the ocean is your god-self;

It remains for ever undefiled.

And like the ether it lifts but the winged.

Even like the sun is your god-self;

It knows not the ways of the mole nor seeks it the holes of the serpent.

But your god-self does not dwell alone in your being.

你們大部分的表現都仍屬於人性，但也有許多部分不屬於人性，就像是一個不定形的侏儒，在霧裡夢遊，尋求喚醒自己的機會。

我現在要談談你身體中的人性。

能夠了解罪與罰的，不是自我的神性也不是霧中的侏儒，只有你們身體中的這個人性才能了解。

我常聽到你們指摘某人犯了過錯，好像他不是你們中的成員，反倒像你們世界中的一個陌生者、一個闖入者。

但我要說，即使是再崇高的聖賢哲人，也不可能高過你們心中人性的最高點；

同樣，即使再多麼邪惡和軟弱，也不可能低於你們每個人心中人性的最低點。

就像一片孤葉，一定是經過整棵大樹的緘默才轉為枯黃，

Much in you is still man, and much in you is not yet man,

But a shapeless pigmy that walks asleep in the mist searching for its own awakening.

And of the man in you would I now speak.

For it is he and not your god-self nor the pigmy in the mist, that knows crime and the punishment of crime.

Oftentimes have I heard you speak of one who commits a wrong as though he were not one of you, but a stranger unto you and an intruder upon your world.

But I say that even as the holy and the righteous cannot rise beyond the highest which is in each one of you,

So the wicked and the weak cannot fall lower than the lowest which is in you also.

And as a single leaf turns not yellow but with the silent knowledge of the whole tree,

所以，若沒有你們心中隱藏的允諾，作惡者也無法胡作非為。

如同一個隊伍，你們一同朝向神性的自我前進，

你們既是道路，也是過路的旅者。

當你們其中一人跌倒時，其實他是為了後面的人而跌，以免他們沒有避開絆腳的石頭。

噢，他也是為了前面的人而跌，因為他們步履雖然更快更明確，然而卻沒有挪開絆腳石。

還有，這話儘管會讓你們心情沉重：

被殺者對其殺人者並非全無責任，

被劫者對其被劫並非無可責難。

行善守法者對於惡人的行為，也並非完全沒有責任，

在作惡者所犯下的罪行當中，就算是無罪者的雙手也未必清白。

So the wrong-doer cannot do wrong without the hidden will of you all.

Like a procession you walk together towards your god-self.

You are the way and the wayfarers.

And when one of you falls down he falls for those behind him, a caution against the stumbling stone.

Ay, and he falls for those ahead of him, who though faster and surer of foot, yet removed not the stumbling stone.

And this also, though the word lie heavy upon your hearts:

The murdered is not unaccountable for his own murder,

And the robbed is not blameless in being robbed.

The righteous is not innocent of the deeds of the wicked,

And the white-handed is not clean in the doings of the felon.

擔。

的確，罪人往往是受害人的犧牲品，但更常見的是，受宣判有罪者，同時也背負了無辜與無罪之人的重擔。

你們不能將公正與不公、善良與邪惡劃分為二；因為它們是站在一起面對陽光的，就像黑、白色兩線互相交織在一起。

當黑線斷裂時，織工則應該觀察整塊織布，同時也應該檢查織布機。

如果你們把一位不忠的妻子送上法庭，應該也用磅秤去秤量她丈夫的心，用同樣的標準去衡量他的靈魂。

讓受鞭笞的犯罪者也審視那受害者的靈魂。

如果你們以公正之名來懲罰犯罪者，用斧頭劈邪惡之樹，讓他也觀察一下那樹的根莖；

Yea, the guilty is oftentimes the victim of the injured,

And still more often the condemned is the burden-bearer for the guiltless and unblamed.

You cannot separate the just from the unjust and the good from the wicked;

For they stand together before the face of the sun even as the black thread and the white are woven together.

And when the black thread breaks, the weaver shall look into the whole cloth, and he shall examine the loom also.

If any of you would bring judgment the unfaithful wife, Let him also weight the heart of her husband in scales, and measure his soul with measurements.

And let him who would lash the offender look unto the spirit of the offended.

And if any of you would punish in the name of righteousness and lay the ax unto the evil tree, let him see to its roots;

事實上，他將發現善根與惡根、貧瘠的根與豐富的根，彼此交纏在大地沉默的心中。

而你們這些想要保持公正的法官，對於那軀殼忠實而精神上是個竊賊的人，將如何判決呢？

對於那傷害他人肉體但實際自己在精神上也受害的人，又將給予何種懲罰？

你們怎麼能告發一個有欺騙或壓迫行為的人，但同時也是受到迫害和凌辱的人呢？

你們又如何懲罰那些充滿悔恨，受到的折磨已超過他所犯下過錯的人？

你們所執行法律所講求的正義不正是為了讓人感到悔恨？

你們無法將悔恨加於無罪者身上，也無法使有罪之人免於悔恨。

And verily he will find the roots of the good and the bad, the fruitful and the fruitless, all entwined together in the silent heart of the earth.

And you judges who would be just,

What judgment pronounce you upon him who though honest in the flesh yet is a thief in spirit?

What penalty lay you upon him who slays in the flesh yet is himself slain in the spirit?

And how prosecute you him who in action is a deceiver and an oppressor, Yet who also is aggrieved and outraged?

And how shall you punish those whose remorse is already greater than their misdeeds?

Is not remorse the justice which is administered by that very law which you would fain serve?

Yet you cannot lay remorse upon the innocent nor lift it from the heart of the guilty.

悔恨將在午夜不請自來，使人驚醒，審視自己。

至於你們這些力圖了解公正的人，除非在一切完全光明中審視行為，否則又怎能了解公正呢？

只在那時你們才能明白，那至善與至惡不過就是立於侏儒的黑夜與神性的白晝之間中的同一個人。

在神殿裡的基石並不會比那最底層的基石來得高。

Unbidden shall it call in the night, that men may wake and gaze upon themselves.

And you who would understand justice, how shall you unless you look upon all deeds in the fullness of light?

Only then shall you know that the erect and the fallen are but one man standing in twilight between the night of his pigmy-self and the day of his god-self,

And that the corner-stone of the temple is not higher than the lowest stone in its foundation.

關於法律

然後,一位律師說:「那我們的法律是怎樣的呢?大師。」

他答道:

你們樂於立法,

但更樂於破壞它們。

如同海邊玩耍的孩子,很有毅力地搭建沙塔,再笑著將它們破壞。

不過當你們建造沙塔時,海洋又送更多的沙子上來海灘,

當你們摧毀沙塔時,海洋也和你們一同哄笑。

的確,大海總是與天真無知的人同聲歡笑。

但對於那些不以海洋、不以人為法律為沙塔的人又該如何呢?

對於那些以生命為岩石,以法律為刀鑿,在石上雕鑿成自身模樣的人,又該如何呢?

On Laws

Then a lawyer said, "But what of our Laws, master?"

And he answered:

You delight in laying down laws,

Yet you delight more in breaking them.

Like children playing by the ocean who build sand-towers with constancy and then destroy them with laughter.

But while you build your sand-towers the ocean brings more sand to the shore,

And when you destroy them, the ocean laughs with you.

Verily the ocean laughs always with the innocent.

But what of those to whom life is not an ocean, and man-made laws are not sand-towers,

But to whom life is a rock, and the law a chisel with which they would carve it in their own likeness?

對於痛恨舞者的殘疾者呢？

對於喜歡牛軛，視森林中的麋鹿為迷途流浪者的公牛呢？

對無法蛻皮、卻稱他人為赤裸和不知羞恥的老蛇呢？

對那些早早赴婚宴，飽倦歸來後卻說一切宴會都是違反法律，所有赴宴者都是犯法者的人又當如何呢？

我該如何說這些人呢？他們也是站在陽光底下，只不過他們都背對太陽。

他們只看到自己的影子，這影子就是他們的法律。

對他們來說，太陽除了投射影子外還有什麼呢？

是要承認法律只是彎著腰，去追隨自己投在地上的影子嗎？

假如你們面向太陽行進，投射在大地上的陰影又怎能約束你們？

What of the cripple who hates dancers?

What of the ox who loves his yoke and deems the elk and deer of the forest stray and vagrant things?

What of the old serpent who cannot shed his skin, and calls all others naked and shameless?

And of him who comes early to the wedding-feast, and when overfed and tired goes his way saying that all feasts are violation and all feasters law-breakers?

What shall I say of these save that they too stand in the sunlight, but with their backs to the sun?

They see only their shadows, and their shadows are their laws.

And what is the sun to them but a caster of shadows?

And what is it to acknowledge the laws but to stoop down and trace their shadows upon the earth?

But you who walk facing the sun, what images drawn on the earth can hold you?

如果你們乘風去旅行，什麼樣的風向標能為你們指示方向？

如果你們不在監獄門前打破枷鎖，人為的法律怎能將你們束縛？

如果你們跳舞而不被任何人的鐵鍊絆倒，還有什麼法律會令你們害怕？

如果你們脫下衣衫，卻沒把衣衫丟棄在無人之徑，誰又會把你們帶上法庭呢？

阿法利斯城的人們啊，你們可以掩住鼓聲，鬆弛七弦豎琴琴弦，但誰又能夠下令禁止雲雀歌唱？

You who travel with the wind, what weathervane shall direct your course?

What man's law shall bind you if you break your yoke but upon no man's prison door?

What laws shall you fear if you dance but stumble against no man's iron chains?

And who is he that shall bring you to judgment if you tear off your garment yet leave it in no man's path?

People of Orphalese, you can muffle the drum, and you can loosen the strings of the lyre, but who shall command the skylark not to sing?

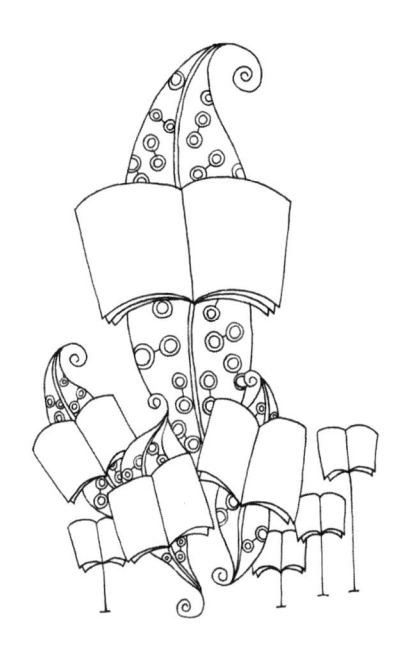

14 關於自由

一位演說家說:「請跟我們說說自由。」

他答道:

在城門邊,在爐火旁,我曾看到你們匍匐於地,膜拜自己的自由,就像奴隸們儘管飽受暴君的戕害,但還要在他面前卑躬屈膝,作賤自己。

唉,在寺廟的樹叢中,在避難所的陰影下,我曾看見你們之間最自由的人,把自己的自由穿戴在身上,如同穿上束縛與枷鎖。

我的心在淌血;只有當你們把尋求自由的願望看成一種束縛,當你們不再視自由為目標和成就時,你們才是真正獲得自由。

真正的自由並不是在白晝無憂無慮,夜晚無所冀求,毫無悲傷。

不過,當這些事物圍繞著你們的生命,而你們超脫它們,直率而解開拘束時,你們更是自由的。

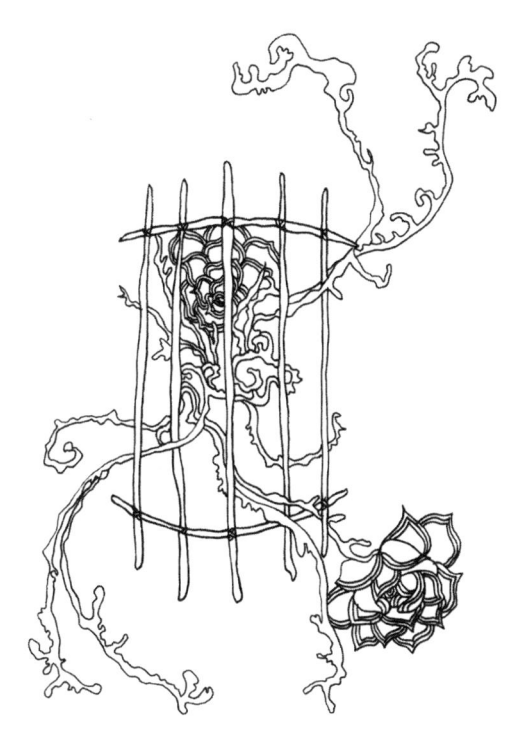

On Freedom

And an orator said, "Speak to us of Freedom."

And he answered:

At the city gate and by your fireside I have seen you prostrate yourself and worship your own freedom,

Even as slaves humble themselves before a tyrant and praise him though he slays them.

Ay, in the grove of the temple and in the shadow of the citadel I have seen the freest among you wear their freedom as a yoke and a handcuff.

And my heart bled within me; for you can only be free when even the desire of seeking freedom becomes a harness to you, and when you cease to speak of freedom as a goal and a fulfillment.

You shall be free indeed when your days are not without a care nor your nights without a want and a grief,

But rather when these things girdle your life and yet you rise above them naked and unbound.

除非你打破那些在你所理解的晨曦之中已經綁住你與午時的鏈鎖，否則你將如何超越你的白晝與黑夜？

實際上，你們所謂的自由正是這些鎖鏈之中最堅固的一環，儘管它的鏈環在陽光下閃耀，迷惑了你們的眼睛。

如果你們對自己有所取捨，不就得以自由了嗎？

如果那是一個你們想要廢除的不公平法律，而這法律正是當初你們親手寫在額頭上的。

你們無法用焚毀律典或沖洗法官的額頭將它抹去，即使你們傾瀉海水清洗。

如果你們想要推翻一位暴君，先看看他豎立在你們心中的王位是否已被摧毀。

And how shall you rise beyond your days and nights unless you break the chains which you at the dawn of your understanding have fastened around your noon hour?

In truth that which you call freedom is the strongest of these chains, though its links glitter in the sun and dazzle the eyes.

And what is it but fragments of your own self you would discard that you may become free?

If it is an unjust law you would abolish, that law was written with your own hand upon your own forehead.

You cannot erase it by burning your law books nor by washing the foreheads of your judges, though you pour the sea upon them.

And if it is a despot you would dethrone, see first that his throne erected within you is destroyed.

如果他們的自由裡沒有暴政，他們的尊嚴中沒有恥辱，暴君怎能統治有自由、有尊嚴的人？

如果那是你們想要擺脫的焦慮，你們可以選擇，焦慮不會強加於你們身上。

如果那是你們想要驅散的恐懼，這恐懼的位置是在你們心裡，而不是在令人感到可怕的對象手中。

的確，你身上所有的東西都確實處於正反對立之中。你所渴望的和恐懼的、厭惡的和珍貴的，追求的和逃避的，莫不是如此。

當陰影消逝不再時，徘徊的光將成為另一道光的影子。

因此，當你們的自由擺脫枷鎖，它本身將會成為更大自由的枷鎖。

For how can a tyrant rule the free and the proud, but for a tyranny in their own freedom and a shame in their won pride?

And if it is a care you would cast off, that care has been chosen by you rather than imposed upon you.

And if it is a fear you would dispel, the seat of that fear is in your heart and not in the hand of the feared.

Verily all things move within your being in constant half embrace, the desired and the dreaded, the repugnant and the cherished, the pursued and that which you would escape. These things move within you as lights and shadows in pairs that cling.

And when the shadow fades and is no more, the light that lingers becomes a shadow to another light.

And thus your freedom when it loses its fetters becomes itself the fetter of a greater freedom.

15 關於理性與熱情

那位女祭司也開口說道：「請跟我們談談理性與熱情。」

他回答道：

你們的心靈往往就是戰場，你們的理性與判斷同你們的熱情與慾望在其中互相交戰。

我多麼希望自己成為你們心靈的和平製造者，將你們心中的不和與競爭成分化為一致的旋律。

但除非你們自身也是製造和平的人，愛著自身所有的成分，不然我該如何做到？

理性與熱情是你們航行中的靈魂的船舵與船帆。

假如你們的舵或帆被損壞，你們就只能任憑顛沛流離，或滯留海中央。

15

On Reason And Passion

And the priestess spoke again and said: "Speak to us of Reason and Passion."

And he answered saying:

Your soul is oftentimes a battlefield, upon which your reason and your judgment wage war against passion and your appetite.

Would that I could be the peacemaker in your soul, that I might turn the discord and the rivalry of your elements into oneness and melody.

But how shall I, unless you yourselves be also the peacemakers, nay, the lovers of all your elements?

Your reason and your passion are the rudder and the sails of your seafaring soul.

If either your sails or our rudder be broken, you can but toss and drift, or else be held at a standstill in mid-seas.

理性一向獨自支配，是一種壓制的力量；熱情一向無所受控，就像火焰燃燒直至毀滅。

因此，讓你們的靈魂將理性提升到熱情的頂點，它將歌唱；讓理性引導著熱情，也讓心靈用理性來引導你們的熱情，日復一日的復活著，宛若鳳凰從自己的灰燼中飛翔。

願你們把自身的判斷和欲望視作家中的兩位嘉賓。

你們自然不會厚此薄彼或另眼看待；因為過於偏重其中一位，都會使你們同時失去他倆的友愛和信任。

在山中，當你們坐在白楊樹蔭下，分享遠方田野與草地的和平與寧靜——讓你們的心在寂靜中說：「上帝憩於理性。」

當暴風雨驟臨，狂風震撼森林，雷鳴閃電宣示了天空的威嚴——讓你們的心在敬畏中說：「上帝行於熱情。」

既然你們是上帝領域裡的一縷氣息，上帝森林裡的一片樹葉，那你們也應當在理性中休息，在熱情中活躍。

For reason, ruling alone, is a force confining; and passion, unattended, is a flame that burns to its own destruction.

Therefore let your soul exalt your reason to the height of passion; that it may sing;

And let it direct your passion with reason, that your passion may live through its own daily resurrection, and like the phoenix rise above its own ashes.

I would have you consider your judgment and your appetite even as you would two loved guests in your house.

Surely you would not honour one guest above the other; for he who is more mindful of one loses the love and the faith of both.

Among the hills, when you sit in the cool shade of the white poplars, sharing the peace and serenity of distant fields and meadows -- then let your heart say in silence, "God rests in reason."

And when the storm comes, and the mighty wind shakes the forest, and thunder and lightning proclaim the majesty of the sky, -- then let your heart say in awe, "God moves in passion."

And since you are a breath In God's sphere, and a leaf in God's forest, you too should rest in reason and move in passion.

關於痛苦

16

一位婦人說：「請和我們談談痛苦。」

他說道：

你們的痛苦正是那破殼而出的領悟。

正如同果核必須破裂，果仁必得暴露於陽光下，所以你們也必須知道痛苦。

你們的心靈若能每天保持對生命奇蹟的讚嘆，你們對痛苦的驚奇便不會比喜悅來得少；

你們將習慣心靈的季節變化，就像已習慣接受來去於田野的季節變化。

於是，你們將能夠透過悲涼的冬季來看待寧靜的心情。

你們的痛苦多半是自己的選擇。

On Pain

Ind a woman spoke, saying, "Tell us of Pain."

And he said:

Your pain is the breaking of the shell that encloses your understanding.

Even as the stone of the fruit must break, that its heart may stand in the sun, so must you know pain.

And could you keep your heart in wonder at the daily miracles of your life, your pain would not seem less wondrous than your joy;

And you would accept the seasons of your heart, even as you have always accepted the seasons that pass over your fields.

And you would watch with serenity through the winters of your grief.

Much of your pain is self-chosen.

它就是你們內心的醫生為了治療你們病軀所給的一帖苦藥。

因此請信任這醫生，平靜地飲下他的藥劑：

儘管他的手，沉重而堅硬，卻是由一隻看不見的溫柔之手指引著。

儘管他端上的杯子，灼傷了你的雙唇，卻是由自己神聖的淚水打濕陶土所捏成。

It is the bitter potion by which the physician within you heals your sick self.

Therefore trust the physician, and drink his remedy in silence and tranquillity:

For his hand, though heavy and hard, is guided by the tender hand of the Unseen,

And the cup he brings, though it burn your lips, has been fashioned of the clay which the Potter has moistened with His own sacred tears.

17 關於自知

一位男子說：「請給我們講講自知。」

他回答道：

在沉默中，你們的心領悟了日夜的奧秘。

但是你們的耳朵卻熱切希望傾聽到你們心靈知識的聲音。

你們想用語言了解你們一向用思考了解的事物。

你們想用手指觸摸你們夢想的赤裸身軀。

這正是你們該做的。

深藏在你們靈魂中的源泉的確需要湧現，淙淙地流向大海；

你們內心中無盡深處的寶藏，將在你們眼前顯現。

但不要用天秤秤量你們未知的寶藏；

也不要用長棒或量繩去測量你們的知識。

On Self-Knowledge

And a man said, "Speak to us of Self-Knowledge."

And he answered, saying:

Your hearts know in silence the secrets of the days and the nights.

But your ears thirst for the sound of your heart's knowledge.

You would know in words that which you have always know in thought.

You would touch with your fingers the naked body of your dreams.

And it is well you should.

The hidden well-spring of your soul must needs rise and run murmuring to the sea;

And the treasure of your infinite depths would be revealed to your eyes.

But let there be no scales to weigh your unknown treasure;

And seek not the depths of your knowledge with staff or sounding line.

因為自我就像是無邊無際、不可度量的大海。

不要說:「我發現了真理。」而應說:「我發現了一條真理。」

不要說:「我找到了靈魂的道路。」而應說:「我遇見了靈魂在我的道路上行走。」

因為靈魂漫步於一切道路。

靈魂不是在一條直線上前進,也不是像蘆葦般成長。

靈魂自我綻放,就像一朵開有無數花瓣的蓮花。

For self is a sea boundless and measureless.

Say not, "I have found the truth," but rather, "I have found a truth."

Say not, "I have found the path of the soul." Say rather, "I have met the soul walking upon my path."

For the soul walks upon all paths.

The soul walks not upon a line, neither does it grow like a reed.

The soul unfolds itself, like a lotus of countless petals.

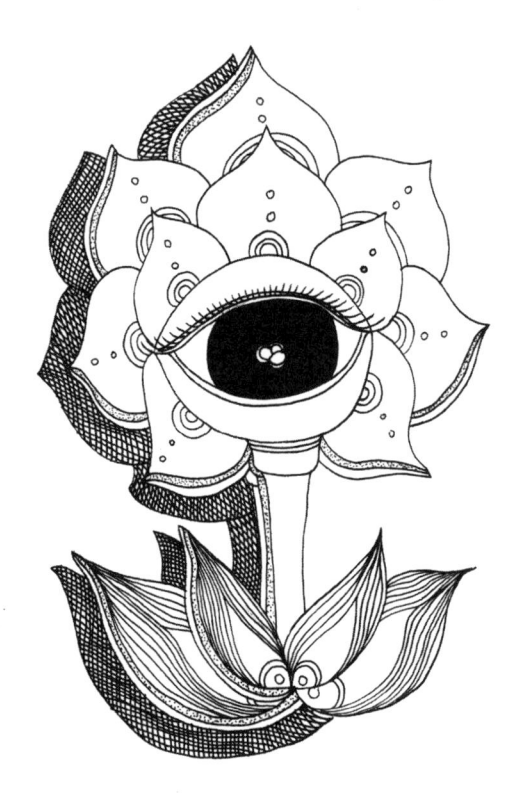

關於教育

然後一位教師說：「請對我們講講教育。」

他說道：

除了在你們知識曙光裡半醒的靈感外，無人能夠昭示你們。

那位走在神殿影子底下和追隨者、弟子們一起散步的導師，給予弟子們的是他的信念和愛，而不是智慧。

如果這位導師真正睿智，便不會命令你們邁入智慧的殿堂，而是引領你們跨入自己心靈的門檻。

天文學家也許能向你們講授他對太空的認知，但卻無法給予你們他的感覺。

音樂家也許唱得出蘊藏於宇宙的旋律給你們聽，但卻無法給予你們捕捉這旋律的耳朵，或回應這旋律的聲音。

On Teaching

Then said a teacher, "Speak to us of Teaching."

And he said:

No man can reveal to you aught but that which already lies half asleep in the dawning of our knowledge.

The teacher who walks in the shadow of the temple, among his followers, gives not of his wisdom but rather of his faith and his lovingness.

If he is indeed wise he does not bid you enter the house of wisdom, but rather leads you to the threshold of your own mind.

The astronomer may speak to you of his understanding of space, but he cannot give you his understanding.

The musician may sing to you of the rhythm which is in all space, but he cannot give you the ear which arrests the rhythm nor the voice that echoes it.

精通代數的人能談論度量衡的領域,但卻無法將你們引向那裡。

因為一個人的觀察之翼是無法轉借給另一人的。

在上帝的知識世界裡,正如同你們每個人是獨立的個體,你們每個人對上帝的認識和世界的理解也彼此獨立。

And he who is versed in the science of numbers can tell of the regions of weight and measure, but he cannot conduct you thither.

For the vision of one man lends not its wings to another man.

And even as each one of you stands alone in God's knowledge, so must each one of you be alone in his knowledge of God and in his understanding of the earth.

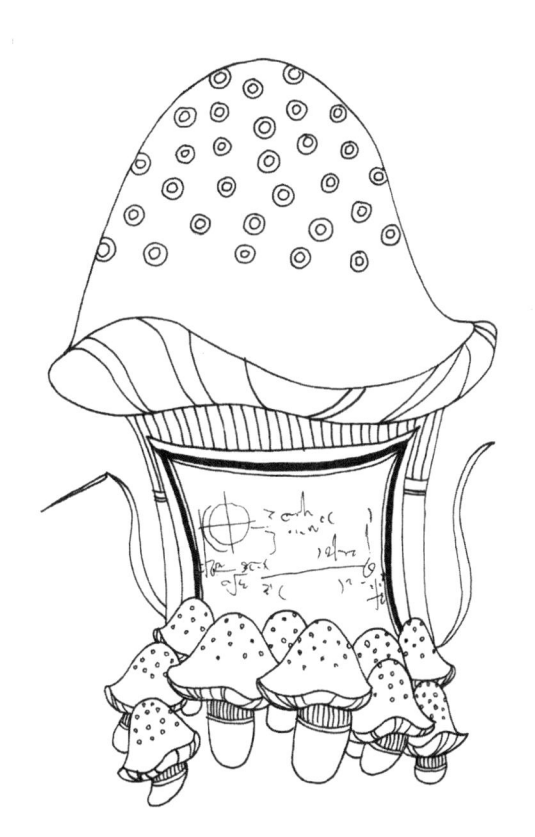

關於友誼

一個青年說：「請為我們說說友誼。」

他回答道：

你的朋友是你需求的解答。

他是你的土地，你帶著愛播種，帶著感激的心情收割。

他是你的餐桌和你的爐灶，你飢渴時奔向他，向他尋求平靜。

當你的朋友傾訴他的心聲，不要害怕自己心中的「不」，也不要隱瞞你心中的「是」。

當他沉默時，你的心仍可傾聽他的心；

因為在友誼之間無需言語，所有的思想、所有的欲望、所有的期盼

帶著無聲的歡樂同生共用。

在與朋友分別時，你也不會悲傷；

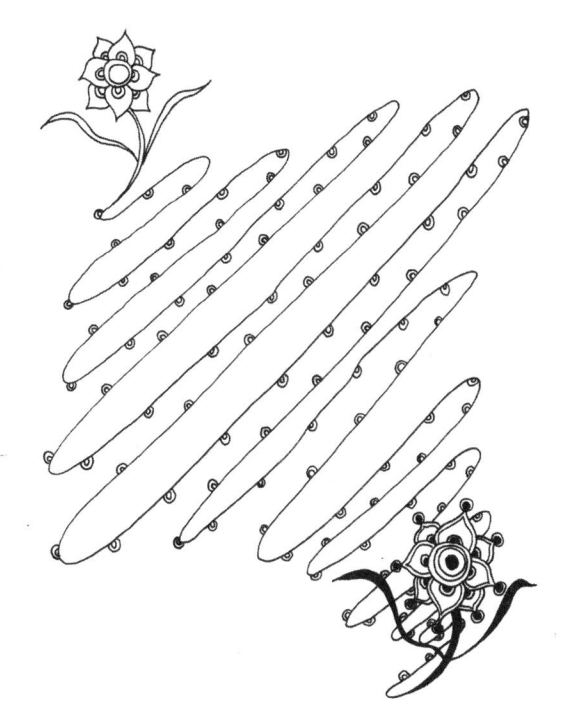

On Friendship

And a youth said, "Speak to us of Friendship."

And he answered, saying:

Your friend is your needs answered.

He is your field which you sow with love and reap with thanksgiving.

And he is your board and your fireside. For you come to him with your hunger, and you seek him for peace.

When your friend speaks his mind you fear not the "nay" in your own mind, nor do you withhold the "ay."

And when he is silent your heart ceases not to listen to his heart;

For without words, in friendship, all thoughts, all desires, all expectations are born and shared, with joy that is unacclaimed.

When you part from your friend, you grieve not;

因為當他不在身邊時,他那些你最喜歡的特質會更加清晰,正如同登山者在平原上望著山峰,顯得格外分明。

除了保留對心靈精神的探求外,不要對你們的友誼別有他圖。

只顧尋求顯露自身神秘的愛不算是真愛,只是一個撒下的網:網住一些無用之物。

奉獻你最好的東西給你的朋友。

如果他必得要知道你的低潮,那麼也讓他知道你的高潮。

只有在消磨時光時才會想去找的朋友,算什麼樣的朋友?

往往是為了要充實生活而去找他。

因為是他滿足了你的需求,而不是填補了你的空虛。

讓友誼的甜蜜中,充滿歡笑和分享的愉悅。

因為在瑣事的甘露中,你的心才會找到自己的黎明而精神煥發。

For that which you love most in him may be clearer in his absence, as the mountain to the climber is clearer from the plain.

And let there be no purpose in friendship save the deepening of the spirit.

For love that seeks aught but the disclosure of its own mystery is not love but a net cast forth: and only the unprofitable is caught.

And let your best be for your friend.

If he must know the ebb of your tide, let him know its flood also.

For what is your friend that you should seek him with hours to kill?

Seek him always with hours to live.

For it is his to fill your need, but not your emptiness.

And in the sweetness of friendship, let there be laughter, and sharing of pleasures.

For in the dew of little things the heart finds its morning and is refreshed.

關於言談

20

一位學者說：「請為我們講講言談。」

他答道：

當你們無法與你們的思想和平共處，你們便開始說話；

當你們無法與心靈的孤寂共存時，你們轉而依附唇舌，而聲音成為一種娛樂與消遣。

在你們許多的言談當中，思想幾乎有一半被抹煞掉了。

因為思想是一隻屬於天空的鳥，只能在語言的牢籠裡展翅，卻不能飛翔。

你們當中有些人因害怕獨處而變得多話。孤獨的沉寂揭露了他們赤裸的自我，於是他們想逃離。

On Talking

And then a scholar said, "Speak of Talking."

And he answered, saying:

You talk when you cease to be at peace with your thoughts;

And when you can no longer dwell in the solitude of your heart you live in your lips, and sound is a diversion and a pastime.

And in much of your talking, thinking is half murdered.

For thought is a bird of space, that in a cage of words many indeed unfold its wings but cannot fly.

There are those among you who seek the talkative through fear of being alone.

The silence of aloneness reveals to their eyes their naked selves and they would escape.

有些人的談話，缺乏知識與先見，去闡述一個他們自己並不了解的真理。

有些人心中擁有真理，卻從不說出口。

在這些人之間，精神都一直存在於沉默的節奏裡。

當你在路邊或市場上遇到你的朋友，請讓心裡的靈魂帶動你的嘴唇，指引你的舌頭。

讓你的言談之音對著他的聆聽之耳訴說；

而他的靈魂將留住你內心的真諦，

如同葡萄酒，當顏色已被遺忘，杯皿已不復存在時，其中的滋味仍長存於記憶中。

And there are those who talk, and without knowledge or forethought reveal a truth which they themselves do not understand.

And there are those who have the truth within them, but they tell it not in words.

In the bosom of such as these the spirit dwells in rhythmic silence.

When you meet your friend on the roadside or in the market place, let the spirit in you move your lips and direct your tongue.

Let the voice within your voice speak to the ear of his ear;

For his soul will keep the truth of your heart as the taste of the wine is remembered

When the colour is forgotten and the vessel is no more.

21 關於時間

一位天文家說：「大師，時間是怎樣的呢？」

他答道：

你們想測量那無法測量且無限的時間。

你們想按時辰和季節調整你們的行為，甚至引導你們的精神之路。

你們願意把時光當作一條溪流，坐在岸邊目送它流逝。

然而永恒對你們來說，就是意識到生命的無窮無盡。

它知道昨日不過是今日的回憶，明日不過是今日的夢想。

因此，在你們體內歌唱和沉思的它，仍依附在將星星撒落在空中那最初一瞬間。

你們之中，有誰不曾感覺到愛的力量雖浩瀚無邊，卻圍繞存在於一體，無法將愛的思緒轉移給另一個，無法將愛的行為轉移給另一個？

21
On Time

And an astronomer said, "Master, what of Time?"

And he answered:

You would measure time the measureless and the immeasurable.

You would adjust your conduct and even direct the course of your spirit according to hours and seasons.

Of time you would make a stream upon whose bank you would sit and watch its flowing.

Yet the timeless in you is aware of life's timelessness,

And knows that yesterday is but today's memory and tomorrow is today's dream.

And that that which sings and contemplates in you is still dwelling within the bounds of that first moment which scattered the stars into space.

Who among you does not feel that his power to love is boundless?

And yet who does not feel that very love, though boundless, encompassed within the centre of his being, and moving not form love thought to love thought, nor from love deeds to other love deeds?

難道時間不就像愛,是不可分割、沒有間隙的嗎?
但你們若認為用時間來劃分季節是必要的,那就讓每個季節都包含在其他季節吧,
就讓今日用記憶擁抱著昨日,用渴望擁抱著未來。

And is not time even as love is, undivided and placeless?

But if in you thought you must measure time into seasons, let each season encircle all the other seasons,

And let today embrace the past with remembrance and the future with longing.

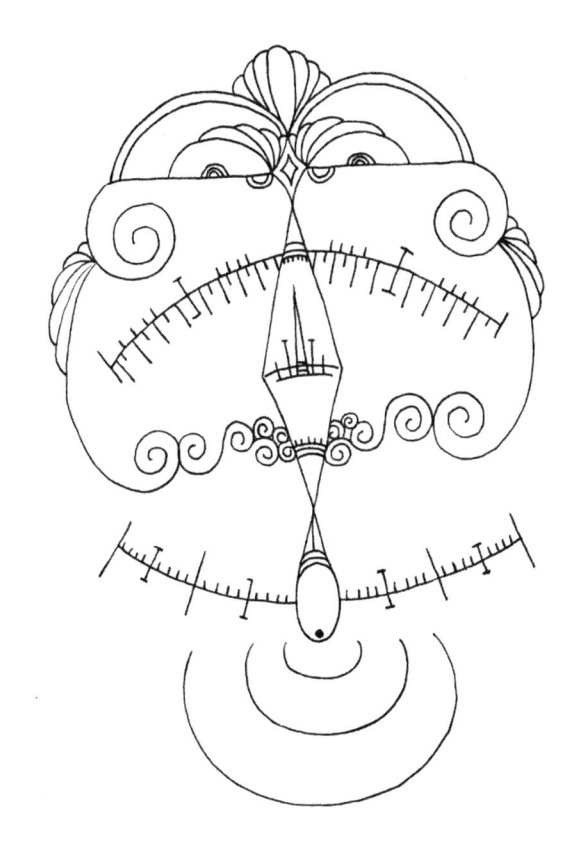

22 關於善與惡

城中的一位老人說：「請為我們說說善與惡吧。」

他答道：

我能談你們身上的善，但卻無法論惡。

什麼是惡？不就是被自己的飢渴所折磨的善嗎？

的確，當善感到飢餓了，即使它到黑暗的洞穴，也會尋找食物；即使是死水，它也會從中取飲。

當你和自己合一時，你是善的。

但當你和自己並非合一時，你也不是惡的。

因為一間分裂的家並非賊窟，只是一間分裂的房子罷了。

即使沒有舵，船隻也只是在岸邊漫無目的地飄搖不定，不至於會沉入海底。

On Good And Evil

And one of the elders of the city said, "Speak to us of Good and Evil."

And he answered:

Of the good in you I can speak, but not of the evil.

For what is evil but good tortured by its own hunger and thirst?

Verily when good is hungry it seeks food even in dark caves, and when it thirsts, it drinks even of dead waters.

You are good when you are one with yourself.

Yet when you are not one with yourself you are not evil.

For a divided house is not a den of thieves; it is only a divided house.

And a ship without rudder may wander aimlessly among perilous isles yet sink not to the bottom.

當你們努力奉獻自己時,你們是善的。

但當你們力求為自己謀利時,你們也不是惡的。

因為當你們力求獲益時,你們也不過是一根依附著土地,盡情吸她乳汁的樹根罷了。

當然,果實不會對樹根說:「跟我學,勇於付出自己的成熟及豐滿的碩果。」

因為對果實而言,施予是一種必需,正如對於樹根來說,接受也是一種必需。

當你們在言談中保持清醒時,你們是善的。

但當你們的舌頭猶如在睡夢中盲目擺動時,你們也不是惡的。

因為即使是模糊不清地講話,仍能夠鍛鍊無力的舌頭。

You are good when you strive to give of yourself.

Yet you are not evil when you seek gain for yourself.

For when you strive for gain you are but a root that clings to the earth and sucks at her breast.

Surely the fruit cannot say to the root, "Be like me, ripe and full and ever giving of your abundance."

For to the fruit giving is a need, as receiving is a need to the root.

You are good when you are fully awake in your speech,

Yet you are not evil when you sleep while your tongue staggers without purpose.

And even stumbling speech may strengthen a weak tongue.

當你們堅定地向目標邁進時,你們是善的。

但當你們蹣跚而行時,你們也不是惡的。

因為即使是那些跛行之人,也並非倒退而行。

不過強壯敏捷的你,可別在不良於行之人面前跛行,還以為那是好心。

你們的善展示於各個方面,但即使你們不夠善時,你們也不是惡的,你們只是閒晃或懶惰罷了。

遺憾的是,雄鹿無法教會烏龜敏捷。

你們對於本身大我的渴求是就存在著善;你們每個心中都有這種渴求。

但你們之中有些人,渴望是一股澎湃的激流,載著山坡的秘密和森林的歌集。

You are good when you walk to your goal firmly and with bold steps.

Yet you are not evil when you go thither limping.

Even those who limp go not backward.

But you who are strong and swift, see that you do not limp before the lame, deeming it kindness.

You are good in countless ways, and you are not evil when you are not good,

You are only loitering and sluggard.

Pity that the stags cannot teach swiftness to the turtles.

In your longing for your giant self lies your goodness: and that longing is in all of you.

But in some of you that longing is a torrent rushing with might to the sea, carrying the secrets of the hillsides and the songs of the forest.

而對於其他人而言，這種渴望是一道淺淺小溪，在抵達海岸前，就已在蜿蜒或回轉中停留下來。

但渴望心強烈的人不要對清心寡欲的人說：「你們何以慢緩而躊躇呢？」

因為真正的善者不會問赤裸的人：「你的衣服呢？」也不會問無家可歸的人：「你的房屋怎樣了？」

And in others it is a flat stream that loses itself in angles and bends and lingers before it reaches the shore.

But let not him who longs much say to him who longs little, "Wherefore are you slow and halting?"

For the truly good ask not the naked, "Where is your garment?" nor the houseless, "What has befallen your house?"

關於祈禱

隨後一位女祭司說：「請和我們談談祈禱。」

他回答道：

你們只在愁苦或需要才祈禱；但願你們在滿心歡喜和日子富足時也會禱告。

因為你們的祈禱不就是你們向生命蒼天延伸的自我嗎？

如果向空中放出你們的黑暗是為了舒緩你們的心情，那麼傾吐你們內心的拂曉，也會令你們愉悅。

如果靈魂召喚你們做禱告時，你們只能哭泣，那麼她也會一再鞭策你們，直到你們破涕而笑。

在祈禱中你們將升至雲霄，從而見到同在祈禱的人，以及那些你們不曾見過，從禱告中獲得救贖的人。

On Prayer

Then a priestess said, "Speak to us of Prayer."

And he answered, saying:

You pray in your distress and in your need; would that you might pray also in the fullness of your joy and in your days of abundance.

For what is prayer but the expansion of yourself into the living ether?

And if it is for your comfort to pour your darkness into space, it is also for your delight to pour forth the dawning of your heart.

And if you cannot but weep when your soul summons you to prayer, she should spur you again and yet again, though weeping, until you shall come laughing.

When you pray you rise to meet in the air those who are praying at that very hour, and whom save in prayer you may not meet.

因此你們對無形神殿的探訪，就成為純粹的欣喜和甜美的交流。

如果你們除了祈求外別無所求，你們將不會被接待；

若是你們只為卑躬屈膝而來，那你們不會因此被提升；

甚至你們是為他人福祉而進入神殿祈求，上帝也不會傾聽。

你們只要進入無形的神殿就足夠了。

我無法用言語教導你們祈禱。

除非是上帝自己引導你們從口中說出的話語，否則祂不會傾聽你們的言語。

我也無法教你們如何向大海、森林和群山祈求。

但你們既然誕生於高山森林和大海之中，便能在心中找到對它們的祈禱。

Therefore let your visit to that temple invisible be for naught but ecstasy and sweet communion.

For if you should enter the temple for no other purpose than asking you shall not receive.

And if you should enter into it to humble yourself you shall not be lifted:

Or even if you should enter into it to beg for the good of others you shall not be heard.

It is enough that you enter the temple invisible.

I can not teach you how to pray in words.

God listens not to your words save when He Himself utters them through your lips.

And I cannot teach you the prayer of the seas and the forests and the mountains.

But you who are born of the mountains and the forests and the seas can find their prayer in your heart,

如果你們在夜靜時仔細聆聽，你們將會聽到它們沉默的言語：

「我們的上帝，你是我們長了雙翼的化身，你的意志就是我們心裡的願望。

是你的願望在我們的體內表達了欲望。

是你驅動了我們，把你的白天和黑夜，變成我們的白天和黑夜。

我們不能向你索求什麼，因為早在我們的需求在心中形成之前，你就已經知道了：

你就是我們的需求；當你奉獻自己給我們時，就已經賜給了我們一切。」

And if you but listen in the stillness of the night you shall hear them saying in silence,

"Our God, who art our winged self, it is thy will in us that willeth.

It is thy desire in us that desireth.

It is thy urge in us that would turn our nights, which are thine, into days which are thine also.

We cannot ask thee for aught, for thou knowest our needs before they are born in us:

Thou art our need; and in giving us more of thyself thou givest us all."

關於喜樂

一位每年造訪城市一次的隱士走上前說：「請為我們談談喜樂。」

他回答道：

喜樂是一首自由之歌，

但它不是自由。

它是你們欲望花朵的綻放，

但不是欲望的果實。

它是深淵對高峰的呼喚，

但卻不是深淵，也不是高峰。

它是鎖在籠中起飛的翅膀，

但空間又沒有被真正包圍。

哦，的確，喜樂是首自由的歌。

我願你們全心地歌頌它，但不希望在歌唱時迷失自己的心。

On Pleasure

Then a hermit, who visited the city once a year, came forth and said, "Speak to us of Pleasure."

And he answered, saying:

Pleasure is a freedom song,

But it is not freedom.

It is the blossoming of your desires,

But it is not their fruit.

It is a depth calling unto a height,

But it is not the deep nor the high.

It is the caged taking wing,

But it is not space encompassed.

Ay, in very truth, pleasure is a freedom-song.

And I fain would have you sing it with fullness of heart; yet I would not have you lose your hearts in the singing.

你們一些年輕人追求喜樂，就好像它就是一切；而他們受到批判和責難。

我既不會批判他們，也不會責難他們。我讓他們自己去尋找。

因為他們尋到的不僅止於愉悅；

愉悅有七個姐妹，即便她們當中最小的也比她美麗。

難道你們沒聽說過一個人在地上挖掘樹根，後來找到了寶藏的故事嗎？

你們中有一些老年人回憶喜樂時感到後悔，彷彿那是一種酒醉後犯下的錯誤。

但後悔只會遮蔽心智，不會受到懲戒。

他們應帶著感恩去回憶喜樂，就像回憶夏季的收穫。

但如果後悔能使他們得到安慰，那就讓他們去吧。

Some of your youth seek pleasure as if it were all, and they are judged and rebuked.

I would not judge nor rebuke them. I would have them seek.

For they shall find pleasure, but not her alone:

Seven are her sisters, and the least of them is more beautiful than pleasure.

Have you not heard of the man who was digging in the earth for roots and found a treasure?

And some of your elders remember pleasures with regret like wrongs committed in drunkenness.

But regret is the beclouding of the mind and not its chastisement.

They should remember their pleasures with gratitude, as they would the harvest of a summer.

Yet if it comforts them to regret, let them be comforted.

你們中還有一些人既非有追求的青年,又非懷舊的老人;

因為害怕追求與回憶,他們躲避一切歡樂,免得輕蔑而冒犯了靈魂。

但喜樂也存在於他們的生活中,

因此即使他們用顫抖的手挖土尋根,也能找到寶藏。

不過請告訴我,有誰能冒犯靈魂呢?

夜鶯會冒犯沉靜的夜,還是螢火蟲會冒犯星星呢?

你們的火焰和煙火會造成風的困擾嗎?

莫非你們以為靈魂是一池可以用一根木棍就攪亂的水?

當你們極力抗拒喜樂時,實際上你們是將喜樂的欲望藏在心靈的深處。

誰知道今天看似被遺忘的,會不會在明天出現呢?

甚至是你們的身體也了解其天然本性和合理需求,而不會被欺騙。

And there are among you those who are neither young to seek nor old to remember;

And in their fear of seeking and remembering they shun all pleasures, lest they neglect the spirit or offend against it.

But even in their foregoing is their pleasure.

And thus they too find a treasure though they dig for roots with quivering hands.

But tell me, who is he that can offend the spirit?

Shall the nightingale offend the stillness of the night, or the firefly the stars?

And shall your flame or your smoke burden the wind?

Think you the spirit is a still pool which you can trouble with a staff?

Oftentimes in denying yourself pleasure you do but store the desire in the recesses of your being.

Who knows but that which seems omitted today, waits for tomorrow?

Even your body knows its heritage and its rightful need and will not be deceived.

你們的身體是心靈的琴弦,它是否奏出妙曲,或者吵雜之音,那全在於你。

如今你們自問:「我們如何從不好的事情中,再分辨出喜樂的好呢?」

走到你們的田野和花園裡,你們將會了解,蜜蜂喜愛採集花蜜而對於花朵來說,很開心能為蜜蜂提供蜜汁。

對於蜜蜂,花兒是生命的源泉,

對於花兒,蜜蜂是愛的信差,

對於兩者,蜜蜂與花兒,施與受的歡樂既是需要,也是狂喜。

阿法利斯城的人們,像花兒和蜜蜂般,在你們的歡樂中好好享受、沉醉吧!

And your body is the harp of your soul,

And it is yours to bring forth sweet music from it or confused sounds.

And now you ask in your heart, "How shall we distinguish that which is good in pleasure from that which is not good?"

Go to your fields and your gardens, and you shall learn that it is the pleasure of the bee to gather honey of the flower,

But it is also the pleasure of the flower to yield its honey to the bee.

For to the bee a flower is a fountain of life,

And to the flower a bee is a messenger of love,

And to both, bee and flower, the giving and the receiving of pleasure is a need and an ecstasy.

People of Orphalese, be in your pleasures like the flowers and the bees.

關於美

一位詩人說：「請和我們談談美。」

他答道：

如果美本身不進入你們之中做為嚮導，否則你們如何能談論到她呢？要如何能找到她呢？

除了她能夠成為你們演說的編織者，否則你們如何能談論到她呢？

委屈而受傷者說：「美是善良而溫柔的。

她像一位全身沐浴著光輝、卻半含羞澀的年輕母親，走近我們的身邊。」

熱情洋溢的人說：「不，美麗是全能而令人畏懼的。

她如暴風雨般憾動我們腳下的土地，撼動我們頂上的蒼穹。」

疲憊怠倦者說：「美是溫柔的低語，在我們心裡訴說著。

「她的聲音屈服於我們的沉默，像一道因恐懼陰影而顫抖的微光。」

25
On Beauty

And a poet said, "Speak to us of Beauty."

And he answered:

Where shall you seek beauty, and how shall you find her unless she herself be your way and your guide?

And how shall you speak of her except she be the weaver of your speech?

The aggrieved and the injured say, "Beauty is kind and gentle.

Like a young mother half-shy of her own glory she walks among us."

And the passionate say, "Nay, beauty is a thing of might and dread.

Like the tempest she shakes the earth beneath us and the sky above us."

The tired and the weary say, "beauty is of soft whisperings. She speaks in our spirit.

Her voice yields to our silences like a faint light that quivers in fear of the shadow."

但好動不安者說:「我們曾聽過她的叫聲在群山之間迴盪,隨其吶喊而來的是雙足踏地、翅膀拍擊和獅子怒吼的聲音。」

在夜裡,城市的看守人說:「美與晨曦將一同從東方升起。」

正午,辛勤工作者和徒步旅行者說:「我們曾看到她透過黃昏的窗邊傾向大地。」

在寒冬,困在風雪中的人說:「她將與春同至,雀躍於山丘之間。」

在酷暑,收割者說:「我們曾看到她與秋葉共舞,雪花飄落於她的髮梢。」

這些就是你們所說的美,然而實際上,你們說的並不是美,而是你們自身未得到滿足的需求。

美並不是一種需求,而是心靈的喜悅。

她不是乾渴的嘴唇,也不是伸出的空手,而是一顆狂熱的心,一個陶醉的靈魂。

But the restless say, "We have heard her shouting among the mountains,

And with her cries came the sound of hoofs, and the beating of wings and the roaring of lions."

At night the watchmen of the city say, "Beauty shall rise with the dawn from the east."

And at noontide the toilers and the wayfarers say, "we have seen her leaning over the earth from the windows of the sunset."

In winter say the snow-bound, "She shall come with the spring leaping upon the hills."

And in the summer heat the reapers say, "We have seen her dancing with the autumn leaves, and we saw a drift of snow in her hair."

All these things have you said of beauty.

Yet in truth you spoke not of her but of needs unsatisfied,

And beauty is not a need but an ecstasy.

It is not a mouth thirsting nor an empty hand stretched forth,

But rather a heart enflamed and a soul enchanted.

美不是你們看到的影像，也不是你們所聽到的歌聲，

而是你們閉上雙眼仍能看見的影像、你們摀住耳朵仍能聽到的歌聲。

她既不是犁痕下樹皮的汁液，也不是與利爪相連的翅膀。

而是一座永遠盛放繽紛的花園，一群永遠翱翔的天使。

阿法利斯城的人們啊，當生命揭開她聖潔面容的面紗時，美就是生命。

而你們就是生命，你們也是面紗。

美是凝視鏡中自己的永恆。

而你們既是永恆，也是鏡子。

It is not the image you would see nor the song you would hear,

But rather an image you see though you close your eyes and a song you hear though you shut your ears.

It is not the sap within the furrowed bark, nor a wing attached to a claw,

But rather a garden for ever in bloom and a flock of angels for ever in flight.

People of Orphalese, beauty is life when life unveils her holy face.

But you are life and you are the veil.

Beauty is eternity gazing at itself in a mirror.

But you are eternity and your are the mirror.

關於宗教

一位年邁的祭司說:「請和我們談談宗教。」

他說道:

我今天所講的,難道不都是嗎?

宗教不就是一切的行為與所有的思考,以及那些既不是行為也並非思考,而是雙手劈石或檢查織布機時,湧入心中的一個奇蹟和顫動?

誰能夠把他的信念與行動分開,或把他的信仰與職業分開?

誰能把時間攤在他面前說:「這份是給上帝用的,而那份是給我用的;這份屬於我的靈魂,而那份屬於我的身軀。」呢?

你們所有的時間都是在天空拍動著翅膀,從一個自我飛向另一個自我。

把道德視作最好的衣裳披在身上的人,還不如赤身露體。

On Religion

And an old priest said, "Speak to us of Religion."

And he said:

Have I spoken this day of aught else?

Is not religion all deeds and all reflection,

And that which is neither deed nor reflection, but a wonder and a surprise ever springing in the soul, even while the hands hew the stone or tend the loom?

Who can separate his faith from his actions, or his belief from his occupations?

Who can spread his hours before him, saying, "This for God and this for myself; This for my soul, and this other for my body?"

All your hours are wings that beat through space from self to self.

He who wears his morality but as his best garment were better naked.

風和陽光不至於使他們的肌膚龜裂受傷。
用倫理道德來界定他人行為的人，就好比將自己善鳴的鳥兒送進鳥籠囚禁。
自由之歌並非從柵欄和鐵網裡傳出。
對於把做禮拜當成窗子一般開開關關的人，必定還不曾探訪他那靈魂之殿；在那裡的窗，日日夜夜一直開著。
你們的日常生活就是你們的神殿和宗教。
不論何時走進，都帶著你們的所有。
帶著犁耙和熔爐，木棒和琵琶。
帶著你們因需要或喜愛而製造的常用之物。
因為在冥想中，你們不可能超越你們的成就，也不可能跌落得比失敗更低。

The wind and the sun will tear no holes in his skin.

And he who defines his conduct by ethics imprisons his song-bird in a cage.

The freest song comes not through bars and wires.

And he to whom worshipping is a window, to open but also to shut, has not yet visited the house of his soul whose windows are from dawn to dawn.

Your daily life is your temple and your religion.

Whenever you enter into it take with you your all.

Take the plough and the forge and the mallet and the lute,

The things you have fashioned in necessity or for delight.

For in revery you cannot rise above your achievements nor fall lower than your failures.

帶著所有人走進祂：
因為在崇拜中，你們無法飛過他們的期望，也不會因看輕自己而降得比他們的失望更卑下。
如果你們想認識上帝，就不要去做猜謎者。
眼觀周圍，你們應不難發現上帝正在與你們的孩子同樂。
仰望蒼穹，你們會看到上帝正漫步雲霄，並且在閃電中張開雙臂，隨雨水而落。
你們應會看見上帝在花叢間向你們微笑，在樹上向你們招手。

And take with you all men:

For in adoration you cannot fly higher than their hopes nor humble yourself lower than their despair.

And if you would know God be not therefore a solver of riddles.

Rather look about you and you shall see Him playing with your children.

And look into space; you shall see Him walking in the cloud, outstretching His arms in the lightning and descending in rain.

You shall see Him smiling in flowers, then rising and waving His hands in trees.

關於死亡

然後阿蜜翠又開口道:「現在我們想向你請教關於死亡。」

他說:

你們想知道死亡的秘密。

但若不往心裡尋找,你們又能在哪裡找到它呢?

就像貓頭鷹一般,只在白晝閉眼、黑夜睜眼,無法揭開光明的神秘面紗。

假如你們真想一睹死亡的精要,那麼請敞開你們的內心讓生命之體進來吧。

因為生與死是合而為一的,正如同河與海一樣。

在你們希望與欲念的深處,靜臥著你們對來世沉默的理解。

就像種在雪地下的種子懷抱著美夢,你們的心也夢想著春天到來。

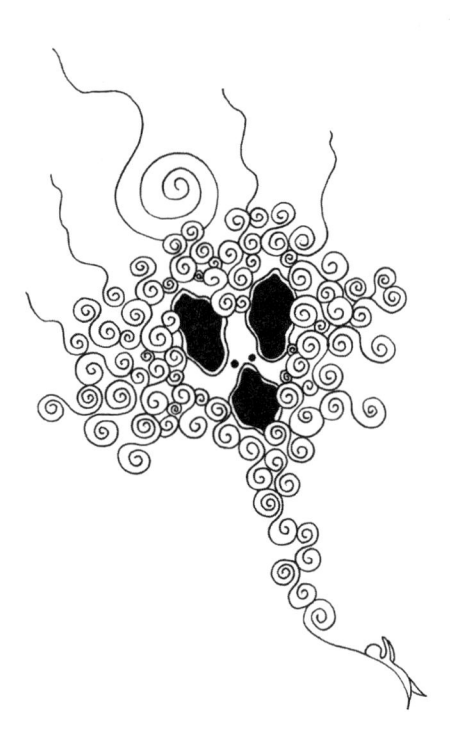

27

On Death

Than Almitra spoke, saying, "We would ask now of Death."

And he said:

You would know the secret of death.

But how shall you find it unless you seek it in the heart of life?

The owl whose night-bound eyes are blind unto the day cannot unveil the mystery of light.

If you would indeed behold the spirit of death, open your heart wide unto the body of life.

For life and death are one, even as the river and the sea are one.

In the depth of your hopes and desires lies your silent knowledge of the beyond;

And like seeds dreaming beneath the snow your heart dreams of spring.

請相信一切夢境吧，因為它藏身於永生之門。

你們對死亡的恐懼，就像站在國王面前的牧羊人的顫抖，而他將被國王的手賜予榮耀。

獲得國王烙下印記的牧羊人，在其顫抖之餘，不也是感到全然的快樂嗎？

他為何不更在意自己的顫抖呢？

死亡不過就是赤裸地在風中站立、在陽光下融化？

停止呼吸不就是讓呼吸從狂奔的潮汐中解脫，使它得以上升、擴展、能夠毫無羈絆地去尋求上帝？

只有當你們在沉默之河中取飲，你們才能真正地歌唱。

當你們已經到達山頂，才能真正開始攀登。

只有讓大地佔有你們的肢體後，才能真正的跳舞。

Trust the dreams, for in them is hidden the gate to eternity.

Your fear of death is but the trembling of the shepherd when he stands before the king whose hand is to be laid upon him in honour.

Is the sheered not joyful beneath his trembling, that he shall wear the mark of the king?

Yet is he not more mindful of his trembling?

For what is it to die but to stand naked in the wind and to melt into the sun?

And what is to cease breathing, but to free the breath from its restless tides, that it may rise and expand and seek God unencumbered?

Only when you drink form the river of silence shall you indeed sing.

And when you have reached the mountain top, then you shall begin to climb.

And when the earth shall claim your limbs, then shall you truly dance.

28 再會

現在已經是晚上了。

女預言家阿蜜翠說:「願今日在此地聽過你話語的心靈都將受到祝福。」

他答道:「是我說的嗎?我不也是傾聽者嗎?」

接著他走下神殿的臺階,人們一路跟著他。待他登上船,站在甲板上。

他再次面對人們,提高嗓音說道:

阿法利斯城的人們!風在催我去。

儘管我不像風這般匆忙,但我不得不走了。

我們這群不停地尋找更孤寂道路的流浪者啊,我們不會在度過前一天的地方開始新的一天;也不會在送走夕陽的地方迎接日出。

甚至當大地沉睡時,我們也在旅行。

The Farewell

And now it was evening.

And Almitra the seeress said "Blessed be this day and this place and your spirit that has spoken."

And he answered, Was it I who spoke? Was I not also a listener?

Then he descended the steps of the Temple and all the people followed him. And he reached his ship and stood upon the deck.

And facing the people again, he raised his voice and said:

People of Orphalese, the wind bids me leave you.

Less hasty am I than the wind, yet I must go.

We wanderers, ever seeking the lonelier way, begin no day where we have ended another day; and no sunrise finds us where sunset left us.

Even while the earth sleeps we travel.

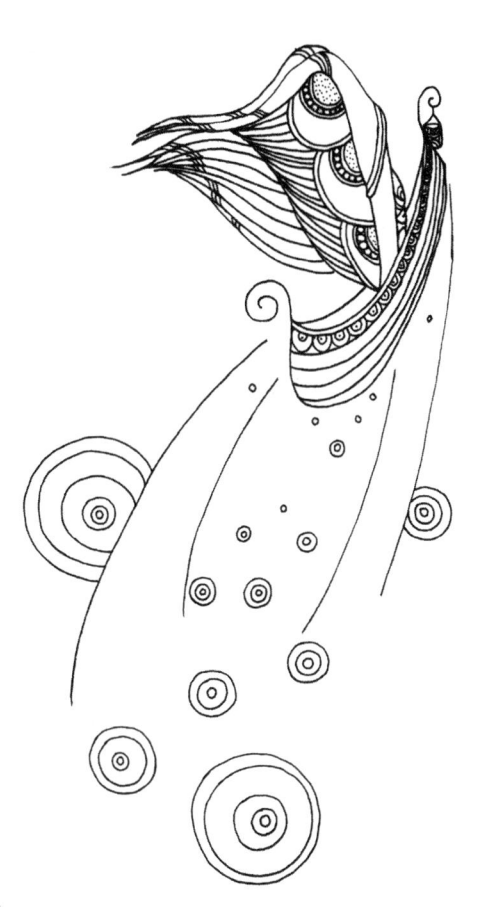

我們是頑強的種子,當我們的心智成熟充實時,就被奉獻給風,飄散四方。

我在你們中間度過的日子非常短促,我向你們說過的話更是簡短。

但在我的聲音逐漸從你們耳邊消逝,我的愛在你們記憶中逐漸消失時,我便會再回來。

我將以一顆更豐富的心和更貼近心靈的唇來說話。

是的,我將踏著潮汐歸來。

也許死亡會將我的身形隱藏,更浩瀚的靜寂會將我包圍,我仍會在此尋求你們的了解。

而我的尋覓不會徒勞無功。

如果我講的是真理,那麼真理就會用更清晰的聲音和更親近你們心靈的話語來呈現。

We are the seeds of the tenacious plant, and it is in our ripeness and our fullness of heart that we are given to the wind and are scattered.

Brief were my days among you, and briefer still the words I have spoken.

But should my voice fade in your ears, and my love vanish in your memory, then I will come again,

And with a richer heart and lips more yielding to the spirit will I speak.

Yea, I shall return with the tide,

And though death may hide me, and the greater silence enfold me, yet again will I seek your understanding.

And not in vain will I seek.

If aught I have said is truth, that truth shall reveal itself in a clearer voice, and in words more kin to your thoughts.

阿法利斯城的人們啊！我將乘風而去，卻並非陷入虛無之中；

如果今天沒有完成你們的需要和我的愛，那麼讓我來承諾某一天能夠實現吧。

人的需要或許會改變，但他的愛不會變，他想以愛滿足需要的願望也不會變。

請記住，我將從更深邃的寂靜裡歸來。

黎明散去的霧留給大地成了露水，升空凝聚化為雲，然後又化作雨水降落。

我與霧沒有什麼不同。

我曾在寂靜的夜晚走在你們的街頭上，而我的精神也曾進入你們的屋裡。

我的心曾感應過你們的心跳，我的臉龐也曾感受過你們的呼吸，我認識了你們所有人。

I go with the wind, people of Orphalese, but not down into emptiness;

And if this day is not a fulfillment of your needs and my love, then let it be a promise till another day.

Man's needs change, but not his love, nor his desire that his love should satisfy his needs.

Know therefore, that from the greater silence I shall return.

The mist that drifts away at dawn, leaving but dew in the fields, shall rise and gather into a cloud and then fall down in rain.

And not unlike the mist have I been.

In the stillness of the night I have walked in your streets, and my spirit has entered your houses,

And your heart-beats were in my heart, and your breath was upon my face, and I knew you all.

是的，我體會到你們的歡樂與痛苦，你們睡眠中的夢也是我的夢。多少次，我與你們就像湖泊與高山，我就在你們之中。我可以像鏡子般映出你們的頂峰和彎曲的山坡，甚至你們的思緒與欲望。

我的靜默裡，傳來溪水中你們孩子的笑聲，河流中你們青年的渴望當它們來到我心深處交匯時，溪水與河流停了下來，也不再歌唱。但比笑聲更甜美、比渴望更深切的東西，也流入了我。就是你們內在的無限；

這是一個巨人，你們充其量就是他體內的細胞和肌肉；他是一位歌者，你們的歌聲對他而言只不過是無聲的顫動。只有在巨人的體內你們才會也變得巨大，通過注視他，我才能夠看到你們，熱愛你們。

Ay, I knew your joy and your pain, and in your sleep your dreams were my dreams.

And oftentimes I was among you a lake among the mountains.

I mirrored the summits in you and the bending slopes, and even the passing flocks of your thoughts and your desires.

And to my silence came the laughter of your children in streams, and the longing of your youths in rivers.

And when they reached my depth the streams and the rivers ceased not yet to sing.

But sweeter still than laughter and greater than longing came to me.

It was boundless in you;

The vast man in whom you are all but cells and sinews;

He in whose chant all your singing is but a soundless throbbing.

It is in the vast man that you are vast,

And in beholding him that I beheld you and loved you.

即便是愛所能到達的距離,是否也無法超越這個遼闊的領域呢?
要擁有什麼樣的洞察力、期許、及假設,才足以飛越那領空?
你們心中的巨人,就像一棵結滿蘋果的巨大橡樹。
他的力量將你們縛於大地,他的芬芳將你們舉至空中,在他的不朽裡你們獲得永生。

曾有人這樣對你們說,你們即便是像鎖鏈,也是整個鏈環裡最脆弱的一環。
這話只說對一半。
因為你們也與最堅強的鏈環一樣結實。
用你們最微小的行為去衡量你們,就好像用最脆弱的泡沫來評估大海的力量。
以你們的失敗評判你們,就像在責怪季節的無常。

For what distances can love reach that are not in that vast sphere?

What visions, what expectations and what presumptions can outsoar that flight?

Like a giant oak tree covered with apple blossoms is the vast man in you.

His mind binds you to the earth, his fragrance lifts you into space, and in his durability you are deathless.

You have been told that, even like a chain, you are as weak as your weakest link.

This is but half the truth.

You are also as strong as your strongest link.

To measure you by your smallest deed is to reckon the power of ocean by the frailty of its foam.

To judge you by your failures is to cast blame upon the seasons for their inconsistency.

的確，你們像大海，儘管嚴重擱淺的船隻等待期盼潮水湧上岸來，但你們就像大海，你們不會催促漲潮。

你們也像四季，儘管在冬季時你們棄絕了春天，但沉睡在你們心中的春天，仍在睡夢中微笑，不以為意。

不要以為我談論這些是為了讓你們彼此說著：「他也讚美我們。他只看到我們的長處。」

我只是將你們自己在心中思考便能領悟的東西用言語表達出來。

透過言語表達的知識，不就是非言語知識的影子嗎？

你們的思想和我的言語，是從我們封閉的記憶中湧出的浪潮，那記憶記錄著我們的過往，

Ay, you are like an ocean,

And though heavy-grounded ships await the tide upon your shores, yet, even like an ocean, you cannot hasten your tides.

And like the seasons you are also,

And though in your winter you deny your spring,

Yet spring, reposing within you, smiles in her drowsiness and is not offended.

Think not I say these things in order that you may say the one to the other, "He praised us well. He saw but the good in us."

I only speak to you in words of that which you yourselves know in thought.

And what is word knowledge but a shadow of wordless knowledge?

Your thoughts and my words are waves from a sealed memory that keeps records of our yesterdays,

記錄了那時大地不知道我們、也不了解她自己的古老日子，也記錄了當時大地在混沌困惑中輾轉不安的黑夜。

智者們的前來能帶給你們智慧，而我的前來是要採取你們的智慧：因為我發現了比智慧更偉大的東西。

那便是在不斷凝聚發光發熱的精神，

你們雖不曾留意過它的澎湃，但它卻為你們的凋零歲月而哀悼。

追求身體生存的生命，才會恐懼墳墓。

這裡沒有墳墓。

這群高山與平地是一座搖籃，是溪中的墊腳石。

每當你們經過祖先的長眠之所，請注意瞧一眼，會發現其實自己和你們的孩子們也正在那手牽手跳舞。

的確，你們常常不知不覺之中作樂。

And of the ancient days when the earth knew not us nor herself,

And of nights when earth was up wrought with confusion,

Wise men have come to you to give you of their wisdom. I came to take of your wisdom:

And behold I have found that which is greater than wisdom.

It is a flame spirit in you ever gathering more of itself,

While you, heedless of its expansion, bewail the withering of your days.

It is life in quest of life in bodies that fear the grave.

There are no graves here.

These mountains and plains are a cradle and a stepping-stone.

Whenever you pass by the field where you have laid your ancestors look well thereupon, and you shall see yourselves and your children dancing hand in hand.

Verily you often make merry without knowing.

也有其他人曾造訪你們，為了得到你們的忠誠，他們許下了黃金般的許諾，而你們則給出了財富、權力和榮耀。

我給你們的抵不上一個許諾，但你們對我更加慷慨。

你們給了我對死後的世界有了更深層的渴望。

真的，對一個人來說，世上最好的贈禮莫過於將一切目的化為乾涸的唇，將一切生命化為一座噴泉。

這就是我的榮譽和報酬——

每當我趨前飲生命之泉時，發現到它本身也是乾枯的；所以當我喝下它時，它也同時飲下了我。

你們中有些人認為我太過高傲或過於羞澀而不願接受饋贈。

我的確自負而不願接受酬勞，但不是禮物。

雖然你們想邀請我入席用餐，但我卻在山間採野果為食，

Others have come to you to whom for golden promises made unto your faith you have given but riches and power and glory.

Less than a promise have I given, and yet more generous have you been to me.

You have given me deeper thirsting after life.

Surely there is no greater gift to a man than that which turns all his aims into parching lips and all life into a fountain.

And in this lies my honour and my reward, --

That whenever I come to the fountain to drink I find the living water itself thirsty; And it drinks me while I drink it.

Some of you have deemed me proud and over-shy to receive gifts.

To proud indeed am I to receive wages, but not gifts.

And though I have eaten berries among the hill when you would have had me sit at your board,

雖然你們想邀我留宿,但我卻已經以廟殿的門廊為床,

然而,難道不是因為你們對我日夜不止的關懷眷顧,使得食物香甜我口,美景縈繞於我夢嗎?

為此我給予你們最大的祝福:

你們付出了這麼多卻不自知。

的確,在鏡中自我凝視的仁慈,最後會變成石頭,

自稱為善行的美名,終究會招致災禍。

你們中有些人以為我很冷漠,獨自陶醉於孤獨,

你們說:「他只理會林中的樹木,卻不理會人類。

他獨坐山巔,俯瞰我們的城市。」

的確,我曾攀登上高峰,走過天涯海角

但若不從高處或遠處,我又怎能看見你們?

And slept in the portico of the temple where you would gladly have sheltered me,

Yet was it not your loving mindfulness of my days and my nights that made food sweet to my mouth and girdled my sleep with visions?

For this I bless you most:

You give much and know not that you give at all.

Verily the kindness that gazes upon itself in a mirror turns to stone,

And a good deed that calls itself by tender names becomes the parent to a curse.

And some of you have called me aloof, and drunk with my own aloneness,

And you have said, "He holds council with the trees of the forest, but not with men.

He sits alone on hill-tops and looks down upon our city."

True it is that I have climbed the hills and walked in remote places.

How could I have seen you save from a great height or a great distance?

若一個人不遠離,又怎能真正地靠近?

你們中的另一些人這樣對我說,並非透過言語:

怪人啊,怪人!喜歡走到高不可攀之處的人,你為什麼要棲息在老鷹築巢的峰頂?

你為什麼總追求那不可能得到的東西?

你到底想網羅的是怎樣的風暴?

你又想在天空中補捉怎樣的飛鳥?

來吧,加入我們吧。

用我們的麵包來止餓吧,用我們的葡萄酒來解渴吧。

他們是在靈魂的孤寂中這樣說著;

但倘若他們的寂寞更深沉,便會了解我追尋的不過是你們歡樂與痛苦的秘密,

我捕捉的只是你們行走於蒼穹之中的大我。

How can one be indeed near unless he be far?

And others among you called unto me, not in words, and they said,

Stranger, stranger, lover of unreachable heights, why dwell you among the summits where eagles build their nests?

Why seek you the unattainable?

What storms would you trap in your net,

And what vaporous birds do you hunt in the sky?

Come and be one of us.

Descend and appease your hunger with our bread and quench your thirst with our wine.

In the solitude of their souls they said these things;

But were their solitude deeper they would have known that I sought but the secret of your joy and your pain,

And I hunted only your larger selves that walk the sky.

但捕獵者也是獵物；因為許多箭飛離了我的弓後，是射入我自己的胸膛。

那飛翔者也是爬行者；

因為我的翅膀在陽光下展開時，投射在地上的陰影就像烏龜一樣。

而我這個篤信者，同時也是懷疑者；

因為我常常用手伸探自己的傷口，這樣我才能因此對你們更有信心，更加了解你們。

我憑著這樣的信任和了解說：

你們不被肉體束縛，也不受限於房屋或田野。

你們居於高山之巔，隨著風飄盪。

它不是一個會爬行到陽光底下求暖、掘洞求安的東西，

而是一個自由自在、環抱大地、周旋於蒼空之中的靈魂。

But the hunter was also the hunted: For many of my arrows left my bow only to seek my own breast.

And the flier was also the creeper;

For when my wings were spread in the sun their shadow upon the earth was a turtle.

And I the believer was also the doubter;

For often have I put my finger in my own wound that I might have the greater belief in you and the greater knowledge of you.

And it is with this belief and this knowledge that I say,

You are not enclosed within your bodies, nor confined to houses or fields.

That which is you dwells above the mountain and roves with the wind.

It is not a thing that crawls into the sun for warmth or digs holes into darkness for safety,

But a thing free, a spirit that envelops the earth and moves in the ether.

如果這些話模糊不清，也不要試圖澄清它們。

含糊和朦朧代表一切事物的開端，而非終點。

而我願你們記得我猶如一個開端。

生命，乃至一切有生命的物體，均在迷霧之中，而非在水晶中孕育而成。

有誰知道水晶不會是那退散的霧？

我希望你們想起我時能記得：

你們身體內看似最虛弱和最惶惑的，其實是最強健且堅定的。

支撐你們的骨骼的，不就是你們的呼吸嗎？

造就你們的城堡，塑造其中的一切，不就是你們都不記得的夢嗎？

如果你們看見那個呼吸的浪潮，你們將不再看見其他事物；

如果你們能聽見夢的低語，就不會再聽別的聲音。

If this be vague words, then seek not to clear them.

Vague and nebulous is the beginning of all things, but not their end,

And I fain would have you remember me as a beginning.

Life, and all that lives, is conceived in the mist and not in the crystal.

And who knows but a crystal is mist in decay?

This would I have you remember in remembering me:

That which seems most feeble and bewildered in you is the strongest and most determined.

Is it not your breath that has erected and hardened the structure of your bones?

And is it not a dream which none of you remember having dreamt that building your city and fashioned all there is in it?

Could you but see the tides of that breath you would cease to see all else,

And if you could hear the whispering of the dream you would hear no other sound.

但你們既看不見，聽不見，這樣也好。

那遮蓋你們眼睛的面紗，將由那編織面紗的手掀起，

堵住你們耳朵的泥巴，將由揉捏它的手指穿透。

於是，你們將會看見，

於是，你們將會聽見。

但你們不應為曾經眼盲或耳聾而悲傷。

因為到了那一天，你們便會了解一切事物隱匿的目的，

你們將感謝黑暗，就像感謝光明一樣。

說完這些話，他環顧四周，看到他船上的舵手已立於舵旁，凝視著揚滿的帆，眺望著遠方。

於是他說道：

我的船長真有耐心，太有耐心了。

But you do not see, nor do you hear, and it is well.

The veil that clouds your eyes shall be lifted by the hands that wove it,

And the clay that fills your ears shall be pierced by those fingers that kneaded it.

And you shall see,

And you shall hear.

Yet you shall not deplore having known blindness, nor regret having been deaf.

For in that day you shall know the hidden purposes in all things,

And you shall bless darkness as you would bless light.

After saying these things he looked about him, and he saw the pilot of his ship standing by the helm and gazing now at the full sails and now at the distance.

And he said:

Patient, over-patient, is the captain of my ship.

風已起，正吹動著帆；

即使錨也在請求啟航；但我的船長仍在靜候我把話說完。

這些聽過大海更宏偉合唱的水手們，也在耐心地聽我訴說。

現在他們不用再等待了。

我已做好準備。

溪流已奔入大海，偉大的母親再次將她的兒子攬入懷裡。

再會了，阿法利斯城的人們！

這一天已經結束了。

它在我們心裡閉上，就像睡蓮閉上等待自己的明天。

我們要保留這裡曾經施予我們的一切，

如果不夠，那我們必須再次相聚，一起向施予者伸手。

不要忘記，我將會回到你們的身邊。

The wind blows, and restless are the sails;

Even the rudder begs direction; Yet quietly my captain awaits my silence.

And these my mariners, who have heard the choir of the greater sea, they too have heard me patiently.

Now they shall wait no longer.

I am ready.

The stream has reached the sea, and once more the great mother holds her son against her breast.

Fare you well, people of Orphalese.

This day has ended.

It is closing upon us even as the water-lily upon its own tomorrow.

What was given us here we shall keep,

And if it suffices not, then again must we come together and together stretch our hands unto the giver.

Forget not that I shall come back to you.

再過一會兒,我的渴望將為另一個人而聚滿塵土與泡沫。

再過一會兒,在風中休息片刻,我將自另一位女子之中孕生。

別了,各位,以及那些我們共同消磨的青春時光!

昨日我們才在夢中相會。

你們曾在我的孤寂中歌唱,我曾為了你們的渴望在空中築起一座高塔。

而現在,我們的睡意已逃,我們的夢已去,亦已不是黎明。

日正當中,我們半夢半醒已度過大半天,我們必須分離了。

假如在記憶的朦朧之中再聚首,我們將再度聚在一起談論,而你們將為我唱一曲更深情的歌。

假如我們的雙手在另一個夢中相握,我們將會在空中搭建另一座高塔。

A little while, and my longing shall gather dust and foam for another body.

A little while, a moment of rest upon the wind, and another woman shall bear me.

Farewell to you and the youth I have spent with you.

It was but yesterday we met in a dream.

You have sung to me in my aloneness, and I of your longings have built a tower in the sky.

But now our sleep has fled and our dream is over, and it is no longer dawn.

The noontide is upon us and our half waking has turned to fuller day, and we must part.

If in the twilight of memory we should meet once more, we shall speak again together and you shall sing to me a deeper song.

And if our hands should meet in another dream, we shall build another tower in the sky.

說話間，他向水手示意，他們立刻拔錨啟航，解下纜繩，航向東方。

人群中發出叫喊聲，像從同一顆心中發出一般，沸騰於空中，如喇叭鳴響，在海面上迴盪。

只有阿蜜翠沉默地注視著船，直到它消失在霧中。

當人們全都散去，她仍獨自立於海堤上，在心中回味著他的話語：

「再過一會兒，在風中休息片刻，我將自另一位女人之中孕生。」

So saying he made a signal to the seamen, and straightaway they weighed anchor and cast the ship loose from its moorings, and they moved eastward.

And a cry came from the people as from a single heart, and it rose the dusk and was carried out over the sea like a great trumpeting.

Only Almitra was silent, gazing after the ship until it had vanished into the mist.

And when all the people were dispersed she still stood alone upon the sea-wall, remembering in her heart his saying,

"A little while, a moment of rest upon the wind, and another woman shall bear me."

國家圖書館出版品預行編目資料

先知／紀伯倫 Kahlil Gibran 著；溫文慧譯
——二版.——臺中市：好讀出版有限公司, 2025.5
面；　　公分，——（典藏經典；68）
譯自：The prophet
ISBN 978-986-178-753-4（平裝）

865.751　　　　　　　　　　　　114003072

好讀出版

典藏經典　68

先知【中英對照新版】

作　　者／紀伯倫
譯　　者／溫文慧
內頁繪圖／三娃
總 編 輯／鄧茵茵
文字編輯／莊銘桓、鄧語蓴
美術編輯／鄭年亨

發行所／好讀出版有限公司
　　　　台中市407西屯區工業30路1號
　　　　台中市407西屯區大有街13號（編輯部）
TEL:04-23157795 FAX:04-23144188
http://howdo.morningstar.com.tw
（如對本書編輯或內容有意見，請來電或上網告訴我們）
法律顧問　陳思成律師

讀者服務專線／TEL：02-23672044 / 04-23595819#212
讀者傳真專線／FAX：02-23635741 / 04-23595493
讀者專用信箱／E-mail：service@morningstar.com.tw
網路書店／http://www.morningstar.com.tw
郵政劃撥／15060393（知己圖書股份有限公司）
印刷／上好印刷股份有限公司
如有破損或裝訂錯誤，請寄回知己圖書更換

二版／西元 2025 年 5 月 1 日
定價：250元

Published by How Do Publishing Co. ,LTD.
2025 Printed in Taiwan
All rights reserved.
ISBN 978-986-178-753-4

填寫讀者回函
獲購書優惠卷